Lamb House, Rye, East Sussex

EMMA TENNANT was born in London and spent her childhood summers at the family's Gothic-style mansion in Scotland. Emerging in 1960s swinging London, she worked as a travel writer and features editor for monthly magazines. In 1975 she founded the influential literary magazine *Bananas*. Her first novel, *The Colour of Rain*, was published in 1963 under a pseudonym. She became a full-time novelist in 1973 with the apocalyptic *The Time of the Crack*, later reprinted as *The Crack*. Many books have followed, including thrillers, comic fantasies, works for children and a series of subversive 'sequels' to much-loved classics. Her interest in archetypal narratives has led her to reinterpret other canonical texts in a characteristic voice blending witty fable, social satire, a feminist analysis of patriarchy and an engagement with divided identity. Made Fellow of the Royal Society of Literature in 1982, she was awarded an honorary D.Litt. from the University of Aberdeen in 1996.

'Emma Tennant has the authentic knack of tapping into one's mental and nervous wiring . . . to read her is to feel oneself in the grip of something as absorbing and impossible not to respond to as a close family . . . One of the strengths of her writing is her thrilling disjunctive oddness. On account of the atmosphere she works up, her fictions are placed in a time that is of our time but not too datingly within it . . . at once violent and cool.'

– Candia McWilliam

'A difficult writer to pin down, Emma Tennant is one of Scotland's best . . . Those who have never read her work may be surprised to discover a voice that was recognizably postmodern in the 1960s . . . If you value the experimental, the surreal, the avant-garde even, or wondered why Scotland never produced an Angela Carter or a J.G. Ballard, Tennant is a writer who will repay your attention . . . Not fitting in, though, is the essence of her work. What truly good writer wants to "fit in" anyway? She has pursued her intellectual passions, rejecting trends and dodging pigeonholing.'

– Lesley McDowell

The
Beautiful
Child

By the same author

The *Beautiful* *Child*

A Ghost Story Based on a Tale by Henry James

EMMA TENNANT

PETER OWEN
London and Chicago

PETER OWEN PUBLISHERS
81 Ridge Road, London N8 9NP

Peter Owen books are distributed in the USA and Canada
by Independent Publishers Group/Trafalgar Square
814 North Franklin Street, Chicago, IL 60610, USA

First published in Great Britain 2012 by
Peter Owen Publishers
Reprinted 2013

ISBN 978-0-7206-1481-7

A catalogue record for this book is available
from the British Library

Typeset by Octavo-Smith Ltd in Constantia 11.5/15
Display Engravers MT
Henry James story Elegant Garamond 11.5/15
www.octavosmith.com

Frontispiece: Jim Linwood
Creative Commons (some rights reserved)
http://www.flickr.com/photos/brighton/2594224331/

Printed and bound in the UK by
CPI Group (UK) Ltd, Croydon, CR0 4YY

To Alan Hollinghurst, with love

PART 1

PART I

PROFESSOR JAN SUNDERLAND

We were sitting around the fire at a house not far from Lamb House, where this story takes place – a house, at least, with the same feeling of space and wide skies as the place the Master had loved, the home of his most contrived and ambulatory fictions.

And because it was Christmas, and the talk turned to ghost stories, we all remembered the same one at the same time, the first volunteer my niece Lou, who was fresh studying Henry James at school. We saw – my sister-in-law Mary and the couple who had rented the Edwardian château and Douglas McGill, the friend of my late brother, as well as an assortment of ladies who crowded on to the sofa as if they knew there was something in the air, something intriguing and even wicked perhaps – we all saw the ghosts of the servants as they appeared at Bly in the famous tale. We shuddered, as if a current of cold water swirled briefly around us. We saw Quint and Jessel and the poor corrupted children; and for a while we sat quiet, as if accepting that nothing more awful could ever be written or recounted.

Then one of the women spoke up. 'There were two

turns of the screw' was offered, in a casual and almost impatient tone, as it comes back to me. 'The horror of young and innocent children utterly *exposed*, as the governess realized at the time, to unspeakable evil. And the hint that she herself haunted the victims: the terrible turn the torturer provides when it's clear that the protector – the source of safety – is the greatest danger of all.'

'Yes . . .' Here my sister-in-law put in her oar, gazing at me for corroboration as she spoke. 'But it's odd that no further turn has come up . . . I mean . . .'

She became a little heated, I thought, and I wished, not for the first time, that my late brother had been there to reassure her, to allow her confidence once more in what she thought, and I said, 'We live in an age far removed from the early years of the last century.'

Mary nevertheless went bravely on. I saw Douglas McGill look kindly across at his friend's wife – widow, I suppose I must call her – but there was too much death already at that evening of the festive season, and I have no wish to recapture that atmosphere now. 'We are surely aware that our world contains the threat of paedophiles, wherever our children may go . . .' And here Mary broke off, seeing the look on her daughter Lou's face – Lou, still so young, not finished with school, Lou who had lost her adored father just two years before. 'That, I suppose, is what I mean,' poor Mary ended, her worried gaze still on the girl. 'That there are things now out in the open which could never be said at the time of the writing of the tale. Things considered too disgusting and shocking to be printed. You know?' And, with a beseeching glance at Douglas and a blush that appeared to settle on her brow and then move downwards to form a fiery ring about her neck, Mary at last fell silent.

But the last thing I could have expected happened next. Douglas, her late husband's best friend, rose and went over to the upright chair (the ladies, as I shall persevere in calling them, had taken the sofa and two armchairs) where my sister-in-law had modestly placed herself after dinner. 'My dear Mary, I must congratulate you on your candour and bravery. For I must tell you . . .' and here he looked around and included us in his audience: not one of us, I saw, refusing this invitation. 'I must tell you,' he repeated and this time let out a sigh along with the words, 'that there is confirmation of what you have told us. A scene of horror impossible to exceed – a tale of perversion and corruption which cannot be paralleled anywhere in the world.'

'But where did it actually happen?' demanded the young woman who had been first to express disapproval at the non-existence of a modern rival to James's ghost story. 'Was it at Bly?'

'No.' Douglas was smiling now, as if determined to humour the outspoken occupant of the deep sofa.

'Are you going to tell us?' Lou asked, her manner a good deal more composed than her mother's flaming cheeks would suggest. 'Was it a house we know about? Are we . . .' And here she laughed as the idea occurred to her. 'Are we in that house now?'

No, McGill assured us, and I saw the quick look of

relief on the face of the young woman who had been most vociferous in her insistence that modern horrors would intensify the effect of James's tale (following my sister-in-law, I may say – but that was Mary's destiny, never to be recognized for an original thought).

'No, the action, if that is an accurate description of a ghost story, took place at the author's home. No country house needed to be invented, no staff or visitors were in search of names. Anyone reading or researching the work of Henry James . . .' And here McGill smiled down at my niece, and I saw the pleasure she felt at being included – in a game, a literary quiz, a ghost hunt, whatever it was, she was likely to be the best qualified in our assembled company that night – and I wished for her, as I had wished for her mother earlier, a small triumph, if only to win over the arrogant ladies on the sofa.

'Yes, Lamb House,' McGill said quietly when Lou, shy as ever, half whispered the name. 'There, in Rye, where the Master had found the house he had always desired – the house and walled garden and the Green Room where he could dictate his great novels . . .'

'But how does a further turn of the screw come into this,' demanded the assembled harpies (as I was now regarding them) now settled ever deeper on the sofa and consuming a tray of dark chocolates. 'Surely he can't have haunted himself,' the outspoken one continued. 'I mean, either you are dead or you are alive and you see dead people. How was it possible – even for Henry James – to be in both states at the same time?'

Now I felt my niece's discomfort at the reference to death and to a haunting uncomfortably close to home, and I looked over at McGill and asked him how this new twist to the famous story had reached him. 'Unless you were visited yourself by the Master,' I said, hoping to lighten the mood of the audience; but Lou, I saw, disliked the subject, and everyone fell silent.

'It is best that I give you the whole story,' McGill said. A sigh of agreement went up, the harpies sat forward to give the teller one more chance, and my sister-in-law Mary even went so far as to say she would sit up all night if necessary to hear the solution of the haunting at Lamb House.

Various voices now rose in expectation. 'It's about an incubus,' suggested Lou demurely – referring, of course, to *Owen Wingrave*, the tale of the boy who, by spending the night in a haunted room, sacrificed his life in order to save his family.

'No, no,' cried the outspoken harpy, and in her excitement the box of bonbons tumbled from her lap on to the floor. 'She was right the first time . . .' And I saw poor Mary blush again at being singled out. 'The haunting must have been to do with a child. Disgusting, pornographic! I can't wait!'

It took several minutes for the general excitement to wear off, and Douglas appeared harried. Suddenly one couldn't help feeling sorry for the man, unaware as he had clearly been of the appetite of the ladies on the sofa for the unspeakable. Once he could make himself heard, I must add, I thanked him silently for defusing the atmosphere – if that is the best way to describe the abrupt change of mood of the company once McGill's need for a postponement was made clear.

There was a lady, It seemed, who had transcribed the whole story of the horrors at Lamb House – and McGill would ensure her testimony would arrive the next day. A friend, an antiquarian bookseller who had been a friend of the lady (she had died at a great age in the 1960s), was expected in the vicinity, staying with friends over the New Year. He would bring a computer disk, and we could hear the tale to our hearts' content.

'Disk?' queried my erudite niece. 'Surely there was no such thing at the time of James's death in 1916? Now how did the story, I wonder, get on disk?'

But McGill was giving away no more. By rising and walking firmly over to his late friend's widow – she took his arm gratefully, I couldn't help noticing, and I saw I was expected to applaud their friendship and possible future marriage I must confess – he had ended the evening.

Or so, at least, he thought. I was unsurprised to see the loud-voiced member of the sofa sorority clamber to her feet and come over to McGill, even going so far as to grab him by the lapel of his distinctly fusty dinner jacket (we were staying in a country house where all the old standards were maintained, and I imagined the retired professor searching anxiously for a tuxedo before rushing to take the train down for the bank holiday).

'So it *is* about children and evil,' insisted the young woman. 'It's just one further turn, then?'

'Oh yes,' said McGill in a tone suggesting that he was taken hostage and must supply this information in return for a rapid escape.

'And what was the child?' McGill's assailant was clearly delighted at being the sole member of the group to hear fresh news. 'A boy or a girl?'

'Oh, neither,' replied McGill with a smile.

'Neither? You mean, the child didn't know?' came back to him. 'What on earth are you saying?'

But Douglas McGill, with my sister-in-law on his arm, had by now pushed out of the room into the hall, and the door closed firmly behind him.

❖ ❖

As may be imagined, I didn't sleep particularly well that night. Our hosts, once breakfast had been dished up (they were a couple retired from media careers, lives of Rolling Stones, women's page editor on the *Telegraph*), were not slow to notice the lack of enthusiasm at the suggestion of either a trip to the sea or to Rye or Sandwich, if we were more in the mood for viewing quaint little houses. Or – in the case of Mary and Lou, who had by now joined me at the breakfast table – the simple sybaritic experience of a new oystery down near the erstwhile home of Joseph Conrad.

'Honestly, Lou, it would do you good,' came from the couple who had been kind enough to suggest a New Year's visit, in return (I must confess) for agreeing a merger with a showbiz literary agency they were about to set up. I – and Mary – would share our knowledge of books, plays and the like with out hosts and in return become shareholders in the company. What could be easier, for my sister-in-law and myself at least? We had lived and breathed literature all our lives, and the older you get in the writing business the more you realize how pathetically little people know about the gems of our civilization. With the exception of Douglas McGill – who could now be seen crossing the hall and making for the dining-room – not one person last night on the sofa by the fire could have identified a page of a classic's prose or correctly named an author.

As if he had read my mind McGill began his day with a reference to Ford Madox Ford and the extraordinary efforts made by Henry James, out on a walk with his secretary, to avoid bumping into him in the meadows near Rye. 'It can't be too far from here,' McGill enthused, while Mary filled a cup with coffee and went over to the window to join him. 'It does amuse, the thought of the Master crouching in a runnel, feet stuck in the bog. Worthy of the pencil of Max Beerbohm, one might find oneself thinking.'

'Max Beerbohm preferred to depict people in drawing-rooms or at parties,' said Lou from her place at table. 'I don't think he ever went outdoors if he could help it.'

'You're right,' Douglas concurred. He marched forward to greet Lou then stopped dead in his tracks. 'My dear girl . . .' and it seemed at first that the garrulous professor was all of a sudden deprived of speech. 'My dear Lou, are you in good health this morning? Are you all right?'

'Come, come, Professor,' our hostess said, in the hope, perhaps, of defusing the look of surprise on my niece's face. 'This is hardly the way to greet a young lady in a country house. When we're here we all revert to being Edwardians, you know. Knickerbockers and flappers apart, of course, we stick to exquisite manners.'

'I must apologize,' McGill said. 'But . . .' and here he looked across at the daughter of his late best friend, his features still showing concern. 'It's just that, Lou, I have never seen you so pale – do forgive me please.' And now, as Lou, further embarrassed by the arrival in the breakfast room of the outspoken leader of last night's sofa brigade, lowered her head and appeared to examine her uneaten toast and marmalade, McGill found himself supported in his comments by our hostess (whose frank stares at the girl were far from the Edwardian etiquette just recently prescribed).

'Lou looks as if she has seen a ghost,' the lady of the (media) manor ruthlessly went on. Then, to Lou herself, 'My dear, why don't we go for a long walk together – through the marshy meadows, if you like, where poor Henry cringed in a ditch rather than get caught by Ford Madox Ford and engaged in con- versation . . .'

'But perhaps she did see a ghost,' said a quiet voice. A smallish man in an ancient tweed jacket had entered the dining-room behind McGill, but the arrival of last night's Ladies of the Couch, a general outburst of talk and the appearance of two further jugs of coffee had obscured him.

Ah, I thought to myself, as this nondescript figure made his way over to McGill and stood looking anxiously up at him (the Professor was at least a foot taller). Here is the story Douglas wishes to entertain us with over the New Year. And – I must admit now, though I was later to change my mind with greater emphasis than has ever occurred to me in my life – my additional thoughts on the subject were hardly illuminating. Good God, are we going to be treated to a watered-down version of *The Turn of the Screw*? I said to myself and barely concealed (for which I must express my regrets to my hostess) the most elephantine of yawns.

As may be imagined, it took an unsurprisingly long time for cups of coffee to be drunk, for toast to be buttered and for the ladies to suppress their innate desire to gossip through everything. Lou, with my assistance, found a window seat where she could sit half-hidden by long looped-back curtains. Mary, blushing slightly, was beckoned to by Douglas McGill and took the next chair to his at the table. Stephen – that was all I heard of the name of the antiquarian bookseller invited by the Professor to bring his 'evidence' of a haunting – stood on a stool provided by the hostess (he would otherwise have been invisible). And finally, to the accompaniment of a soft curtain of snowflakes beyond the dining-room window, the audience fell quiet.

In this great Edwardian house, with all its expanse of glass and imitation oak furniture and its overbearing arrangements of framed photographs and gleaming pianos, my fifteen-year-old niece Lou was the only member of the audience to recognize the name of the author of the paper about to be read out.

'Theodora Bosanquet,' began my niece, 'was the successor of Mary Weld as amanuensis to Henry James – his typewriter, as the job was known in those days.'

There was bound to be laughter at this – and, sure enough, from the direction of the low pouffe where the ladies had finally settled themselves, it came. 'Type-writer – I must say I wouldn't have liked to be known as that,' exclaimed the Leader of the Yamamoto-clad Pack. 'It would make one feel like a machine.'

Lou, I was glad to see, paid no attention to this witty comment and continued with the facts. Miss Bosanquet had entered the employment of Mr James in the autumn of 1907 at Lamb House, Rye. She had mastered – here I saw McGill smile at the use of a word so strongly connected to the famous author, and his young antiquarian friend looked flustered as he ruffled his pages, waiting to read – she had learnt to type at speed on the Remington within little more than seventeen days of the commencement of her employment there.

'So what did she look like?' demanded not one of the ladies, as you might expect, but the hostess in charge of this great architectural disaster herself. 'How did she go down with the great man then? Most men have affairs with their secretaries. Could she have tempted one such as Henry James to fall for her charms?'

'Yes, do tell us – it's her ghost we're going to be told about, aren't we?' (This from one of the young ladies of the night before. More soberly dressed than the rest, perhaps she wanted to be seen as intelligent. McGill, I noted, gave her a patronizing smile.)

'Miss Bosanquet was in her early twenties when she was engaged by James to take dictation of his novels,' Lou said. 'You ask what she looked like, and I expect you'd like to know what she wore?'

'Yes, yes,' said several of the pouffe-seated harpies. Clearly Lou's sarcastic tone had been lost on them, and they envisaged Edwardian corsets, huge skirts and flower-and-fruit-laden hats: a ghost in fancy dress with no resemblance to the young woman who worked so assiduously for the great writer until his death in 1916.

'Miss Bosanquet favoured tweed jackets and skirts,' Lou said solemnly. 'Her appearance was described by Mr James as boyish.'

'Oh, that explains it!' cried my tasteless hostess. For the first time I wished we hadn't agreed to do business with her: I could see the woman would make a travesty of anything she got her hands on, and I dreaded *The Turn of the Screw* which she had proudly said would be put on as a 'counter' to the Aldeburgh Festival next summer.

'Henry James was bi, no?' This query came on the minuscule screen of what must undoubtedly have been the smallest and most expensive mobile phone ever made. (I, as a Luddite, as I believe we're called by the denizens of this Brave New World, took some time to realize I had been texted – the difference between the usual process and this one being that Miss Harrods Couture herself still held the gadget in her outstretched hand. The words showed black against the grey background.)

'Bi,' she shouted at me and, receiving no answer, directed her attentions to Douglas McGill. 'Bi usually means gay, no?'

But the good professor, I was unsurprised to see, refused to be drawn. I wondered at a lack of cancellation of the whole event, once it was known who and what the other guests had turned out to be – but then I remembered that the modest young antiquarian, with his rare books in Bell Street in Paddington and his earnest desire to contribute to the study of English literature, could not have been put off – without a charge of unkindness laid at McGill's door, certainly. And McGill was a warm-hearted man.

'Yes, Miss Bosanquet herself entrusted this account of the dictation she received from Henry James to my uncle at the bookshop,' our guest reader now informed us. 'As late as 1963 – indeed it was at the time of the Lady Chatterley trial, as my uncle recalled, his friend Theodora Bosanquet deposited with him the latest novel from the voice of the Master . . .'

'The year 1963?' Even McGill, who had presumably been unaware of this claim, was unable to conceal his incredulity. 'My dear Stephen, as you must know as well as anyone, Henry James died in 1916. How can you possibly believe that Miss Bosanquet was not also the possessor of this knowledge? Was she . . .' and here McGill's voice faltered, as if he had become suddenly aware of the possibility of forgery, of plagiarism, of some kind of damaged goods being on offer here: shocking even to customers of so low an intellectual calibre as the Pouffe and Ottoman Ladies and (I regret to say) as our own hosts in the Media Fortress.

Stephen, in his battered jacket and with his wispy brown-grey hair now more disarranged than ever, did, all the same, hold out against the professor's charge, implicit only at this stage, of dishonesty. 'Miss Bosanquet continued to take dictation from Henry James for decades after his death,' the bookseller said bravely – but in so low a voice that there was a general scramble from low floor seating to a table surrounded by hard chairs, so the opulently furnished drawing-room of the mock castle resembled, all of a sudden, a school room.

'A gay ghostwriter, a woman known as a typewriter – what more can be coming our way?' cried our hostess delightedly. 'Next we'll be told that the books from another world will be bound in ectoplasm.' And after a spurt of hearty laughter she proceeded to ask in the most serious of tones whether this Miss Theodora had also a haunted Remington which conveyed the deathless prose of the Master as proof that genius cannot die – something in that vein at least.

But the ladies, I noted, now hung on the words of the

antiquarian from Bell Street and began to scribble on notepads – as if a book club meeting or readers' group was under way and they could discover the meaning of life as well as (just possibly) finding a future husband – though on this occasion, with the exception of McGill and myself, no bachelors were in evidence.

'Yes,' said Stephen, whose confidence had grown, I was pleased to see, since the interest of at least six ladies had become clear to him. 'The Remington was succeeded, after the death of the great writer, by an Ouija board. Miss Bosanquet transcribed his tales and novels from this – in her flat in Chelsea,' Stephen added modestly, as if the proof of an earthly abode would convince his listeners of the reality of his strange account.

'But what of the child?' the leader of the newly baptized Literary Ladies pressed him. 'We were told that something more corrupt . . .'

'Evil,' put in the soberly dressed girl who had been jotting furiously on her pad. 'We expected a story of . . .'

'Spirits,' put in my hostess's sceptical and not very appealing husband, the owner of the Media Mansion. 'Which reminds me . . . What would you all say to a shaker of Bloody Marys? Isn't it better than going out for a walk in the marsh in this kind of weather?'

I suppose I can say that I expected a roar – or a sigh, given the affected manners of most of the participants in this search for a further turn of the tormentor's screw – a cry, anyway, of agreement at their host's suggestion of a good strong drink. Yet – and I expect any reader worth their salt could have foreseen this – the entire room now hung on the words of Stephen and his tale of old books. Faith in the authenticity of his and Miss Bosanquet's testimony was unshakeable. It says a lot about the power of stories and the need for narrative – something of the kind.

'The child,' McGill said, rather pedantically I thought. Why must he answer every question? What is the sense of making a bunch like this into a tutorial group for undergraduates? Academics are like that. But I had no desire to halt the momentum of the strangest tale I ever heard told any more than Professor McGill did. It was just that he felt his duty lay in the expounding of theories to anyone he saw.

'Last night we were told there was no child,' said the serious one in grey – and for a moment I saw her as Jane Eyre, escaped from her bad education and the following addiction to shopping. 'So is there – or isn't there, please?'

'In a way.' McGill hedged his bets.

'But whose child was it – if it did exist?' demanded my stand-in for a governess. 'And what sex was it anyway?'

'Oh yes,' said the soft-voiced Stephen, and now he held the crumpled pages up nearer to his eyes. 'Miss Bosanquet's account with inform us . . .'

'Of the gender?' insisted the leader of our surprising new group.

'Oh, that was for her predecessor to decide,' Stephen replied. Then he began to read.

PART II

MISS THEODORA BOSANQUET, 1950

It was a question of revisiting the past, I suppose, and finding it so utterly – so irredeemably – different from the present that only the sight of a small face peering from a window in the house I had once known so well could return me to my years as amanuensis to the great Henry James.

It was Russell Noakes: he was the owner of that small face, of course he was; and he ran – I always remember him running – to greet me as if my absence had been brief instead of the thirty-five years that had elapsed since I left Rye for the last time. It had been a sad, half-demented period when the Master was ill and rambled in his dictation, and we had known for some months that he must return to London, to his doctors – and the illness that would finally carry him away. The diminutive 'houseboy', as my colonially raised predecessor Mary Weld had labelled Noakes – this on the occasion of my 'taking over' as guardian of the words of Henry James – seemed as unaware of the passage of time as I was acutely conscious of it. The railings in front of the house had been stripped away as part of the recent war effort, and though the Master's one-time residence had been acquired by the National Trust there was no evidence of renovation – though on the upper floor from which Noakes had espied me a pot of white paint balanced vertiginously on a window sill and a brush more reminiscent of a child's small paintbrush than of the serious, sensible utensil required for beautifying the exterior of a fine building such as this poked out of a milk bottle at its side. It was a shame, really, that the years of my absence from the house, which ran from a period of Edwardian opulence to the era of austerity following the cessation of hostilities, had used the former home of the world's greatest writer so badly. I knew, of course, that an infinitely inferior author, E.F. Benson, had been owner after the Master's death of this shrine to imagination and perseverance. But somehow Lamb House had not benefited from his occupancy: the place was, quite simply, a wreck.

∴ ∴

So this account, penned by one who has suffered the fears and dangers of a haunting, may dwell, despite my best intentions, on the changes visible in my own appearance, thanks to the passing years; and perhaps because the dwarf-like Noakes, on leaping from the front door and maintaining a steady trot as he came up to me, hand outstretched, exclaimed that I was just as he remembered me, so that I suffered an overwhelming sense of the atmosphere of those past days and saw myself this time – and to my indescribable horror – as a revenant.

Readers of this slim pamphlet will need to know what took me more than a third of a century to try to forget; and what, at the same time, my dreams were unable to resist portraying. Those who become engrossed in the story (if any) will find their chief interest lies in the fact of the presence of the Master at every twist and turn in the tale: both the conceiver and the subject of this odd sketch, his heroism and – I fear to confess – his occasional cowardice haunt the pages more surely than any spectre got up by a mediocre writer. (T. Bailey Saunders, inexplicably a friend of James, comes to mind, but he is not yet ready to be explained.)

So I address those 'Jamesians' who survive the efflorescence of the second rate since the War and know the Master and revere him – though in either department they cannot and never will equal my expertise in identifying a sentence from a novel or a line from a much-maligned drama, *Guy Domville*, a play that caused James much grief.

I came to Lamb House in 1907. My memoir, published by Leonard and Virginia Woolf in the Hogarth Press, gives the details of my arrival as a day in October (I had to return to London for a few days as an aunt was ill and temporarily needed attention, so the exact date of the start of my employment is uncertain). I have described my slight surprise at the lack of interest Mr James demonstrated in his wardrobe – for I had expected a perfectly turned-out gentleman. But genius makes its own rules, evidently, even when it comes to

the owner's dress sense or lack of it. I will not forget my
surprise at the genial yellow of the checked waistcoat
and the jacket which rode noisomely over it. (Astute
readers of my slim volume of reminiscence will detect
that I, too, Theodora Bosanquet, am a writer, though I
lacked the courage in the Master's lifetime to confide my
secret ambition to him.) The small leatherbound work
in which I set out life at Lamb House in the early years
of the twentieth century is not the sole constituent of
my *œuvre*. I have no intention of going down in history
as a compiler of inventories. But readers appear more
titillated by the number of secretarial tables set out
ready for Mr James's inspiration in this delightful old
house than in my memories. There were eight. I do not
write to provoke criticism of an artist so revered, so – by
the time I succeeded Miss Weld – so *worshipped*, one
might say, by the discerning, the highly educated, the
sensitive who made up the readership of the late Henry
James. Some, the more vulgar you might say, can wonder
at the need for these tables in every room and on each
landing: surely, as the Master dictated his pieces, he
could hold the proper word as a diver can hold his
breath, admittedly only for a short amount of time – but
for long enough to allow a gentle walk (out of the
Garden Room and round the walled garden, say) and
back again to continue dictation? But no – as only I
know and instinctively understood from the very first
day of my engagement at Miss Petheridge's Secretarial
Bureau in London – there must on no account be any
impediment to the Great Writer's flow. To lose his place,

as one might put it, could endanger the whole delicately balanced vast construction of his sentences. To suggest a word at those rare times when the correct one had eluded him would be the equivalent of dropping a stitch in the knitting of a multi-coloured magnificent scarf. But here I digress – I wish only to emphasize that Miss Weld (who did not experience the good fortune, despite her wealthy family, of becoming, as I did, a graduate of University College) had clearly expected, on the occasion of my meeting her at Lamb House, an expression of astonishment at the carefully prepared tables, and I made none. 'You will find Mr James's voice melodious,' this young woman had gone on to inform me. And I remember wondering briefly whether a secret passion had grown up, as the handsome Miss Weld traipsed after her employer on one of his more ambulatory days. But this thought was soon dismissed. No plot devised by the Master, either then or now, would be so banal as to incorporate the *amours* of a typist and her dictator.

So it was that I found myself back at Lamb House – or, rather, Lamb House with all the magic gone from it and the low-statured Russell Noakes running ahead of me while spouting his own life story. He had applied to the National Trust and had been appointed as caretaker. There was no news yet of refurbishment or the loving care the historic building would need. There was simply the memory of the distinguished residence to keep one going, with Noakes like a moving key on a typewriter as he jumped ahead from room to room. (The tables had all gone, of course; but the thought of eight bureaux groaning with the work of E.F. Benson was enough to make this far from regrettable.)

Now, as we entered the Green Room, where Mr James spoke his work in winter – there was less room than the Garden Room for pacing or walling up a complex much thought-over story, but it was, quite simply, warmer than downstairs – my dwarf guide stopped abruptly in his tracks and placed his finger on his lips. In the sudden silence the house seemed even colder and less inviting than before, and I found myself shivering, as if some part of me knew that we had entered dangerous territory.

'I suppose all members of the old staff have not come back here to serve the memory of the late Master,' I asked in as jocular a tone as possible. 'The house-keeper, Mrs Paddington – is she . . . still with us, or even perhaps in the pantry now, setting out the cakes?' I knew as I spoke that there was no question of finding dear Mrs Paddington here – she who had worked miracles with the tradesmen's books in reducing the Master's outgoings. Henry James was not rich. The housekeeper and butler in service at the time of Mary Weld's engagement, Mr and Mrs Smith, had apparently done the opposite, changing water, as it were, into wine, but Mary Weld, shocked by a certain episode at the start of her time here, would vouchsafe no more than that.

Russell Noakes shook his head and remained silent. Standing on the parquet before me, I was reminded of a surly child. 'I've come to find something,' I continued to address the little houseman. 'It will be in Mary Weld's desk – in her private study. Can you take me there, please?'

I turned my head to the right and left, as if demonstrating to an idiot that the object I sought must be in one clearly signposted direction.

But I must have closed my eyes, if only for a wink for – as I focused on the dear old room, with its panelling and the shy creeper for ever at the window and the noble fireplace against which the Master had leant so often, in his painful search for a missing word – I saw there was no one there now: Russell Noakes had gone. What was probably a scratching behind the wainscot had me hoping for a second that the kindly housekeeper was here after all – even that Noakes had run off to find her. Yet I knew I had heard no footsteps. The room had grown unbearably cold. I was alone in Lamb House, and a winter evening darkened in the sky before the fulfilling of a day.

PROFESSOR JAN SUNDERLAND

The audience at my hosts' opulent rented château had changed during this brief reading by the young-old messenger from Bell Street. Most of the fashionistas, as I believe their strange race of banters and bulimics are known – both these terms supplied by my niece Lou on a previous trip to Canterbury to introduce her to the *Tales*, the tapestries and the treat (even if she had outgrown it somewhat) of Eggs Benedict at a pretentious little restaurant – most of the young ladies had gone, leaving a table and empty chairs. My hard-working Jane Eyre type, unsurprisingly, remained: after all, something new about Henry James might come out of our time together here, and she could bring it up at her book-club meetings: everyone, at least, had heard of *The Turn of the Screw*.

The other 'student' determined to stick out even the halting feeble-voiced reading from the visiting biblio-mane *was* surprising: the flamboyantly dressed leader of the group that was now dispersed and hurrying frantically to London to visit the January sales: my *bête noire*, as I had privately named her, who now stared across the room at me with an intensity which, had I chosen to match it, could have resulted in a gaol sentence for sexual harassment.

And, yes, my sister-in-law was still here and allowing, so I perceived, the over-attentive Douglas McGill to shift his chair every few minutes nearer to hers (I decided to ignore this, but I confess I was not pleased).

Then there was my rollicking hostess and her bitter-looking husband. What were they making of this strange deposition? I wondered. Could it join the list of Summer Reads on television? Or would it be held over until the festive season when horror takes possession of the bookshop shelves and people gaze into the black hole of a seasonal despair? Was it a ghost story anyway?

'Is this meant to be frightening?' my *bête noire* demanded. She was faultless when it came to picking up the concerns or anxieties of those around her. My hostess rolled her eyes, as Salome (so I named my overdressed enemy) went on relentlessly. 'I mean, is this Miss Bosanquet trying to act out the part of the governess in *The Turn of the Screw*? Is the disappearing servant supposed to signify her hysteria – or what?'

As I was handing a silent if reluctant compliment to the mini-clad, high-booted nightmare, I saw in the bay window the sight I had tried to persuade myself over the past evening and morning that I would never see. McGill's hand – a largish white hand with a faint nicotine blush – landed on my sister-in-law's lap. It wriggled up to the knee and sat there, as if awaiting instructions.

'Surely,' said my Jane Eyre at Lowood lookalike, 'Miss Bosanquet was simply about to inform us that, as a member of the Institute of Psychic Research, she was more able than most to recognize a manifestation from the other side. If our reader would kindly continue, I am positive we shall understand what Miss Bosanquet saw – or didn't see . . .'

It was then, looking over to the pale secondhand book dealer, that I felt sympathy – if only in the most superficial sense – with the typist's reaction to the disappearing Russell Noakes. Oh, I saw the preservationist of the ex-amanuensis's manuscript all right: his mousy hair, white at the sides, his unappealing, fusty corduroys – but I saw for the first time, too, that the curved window seat with the looped curtain, which had on the previous evening almost entirely concealed my niece Lou, was definitely not occupied by her now. The unpleasant realization that McGill's surreptitious and then increasingly obvious movements had released the curtain from its sash shocked me, just as the poor typist must have been when confronted by the sudden desertion of Lamb House by Noakes. Where could Lou be? It would have been most unlike her to stay in bed all morning . . . and she had wanted to continue the 'exploration', as she named it, of a possible ghost story to surpass Henry James's own.

'Miss Bosanquet was told to go to Rye to recover a manuscript left by her predecessor, Mary Weld,' said Mr Bell Street – and, seeing no objection to his continuing the reading, he lifted the recently deposed pages, shifted on the reproduction art deco stool that formed his podium and cleared his throat.

'Why don't we accept the sad truth about Miss Bosan-quet,' came McGill's unwelcome but unfortunately authoritative voice from the bay-window seat. 'It is a known fact that dear Theodora, despite her university education, believed in spooks. She sent you a book, Stephen, did she not? *The Earthen Vessel* by Pamela Grey, one of those tiresome spirit-seekers who made up to Sir Oliver Lodge after the Great War. What we need to know is whether our aspirational amanuensis found anything new by the Master during her visit to Lamb House.'

If we had not been joined at precisely that point by a couple, both middle-aged and fair-haired, who tiptoed into the long vaulted dining-room, thus disturbing proceedings radically (tiptoeing, to my mind, is invariably aggressively meant), I daresay I would have found myself rising and going over to confront McGill. He would have been doubly confounded, I have no doubt, at my reminder that an audience had gathered to hear a new ghost story spun from an old one; and by my intended air of stupefaction at seeing his hand on my sister-in-law's knee (for there it remained, I am sorry to say).

As it was, introductions were noisily conducted by our hostess. Mike and Jasmine had driven down from Edinburgh and been delayed by heavy snow. Mike taught creative writing at Manchester, Jasmine mumbled something about being on a PR trip for her novel – but either I misheard her or her reference to spiritualism in Brontë, a paper entitled 'Jane! Jane! Jane!' appeared to be the chief reason for her invitation to this East Sussex crenellated ghastliness. She and her husband had arrived with the impeccable bad timing found in inferior writers: you could see she was a gusher of an unstoppable stream of consciousness, while Mike lay silent around a crushing and final full stop.

'You haven't missed much,' shrilled our party-giver, as the probability of this couple having been invited to meet me with an eye on future culture programmes began to sink in. 'And may I introduce Mr . . . Mr Paddington . . .'

It was annoying to find oneself laughing along with Doug McGill at this clanger. Not many people, after all, knew or remembered Henry James's housekeeper to have been a Mrs Paddington: she had replaced the appalling Mr and Mrs Smith after the débâcle of a luncheon party in 1902. My irritation was increased when I saw that our shared laughter appeared to have lent confidence to McGill's hand, which had now crept behind the bay-window seat and gripped my sister-in-law by the waist. The antiquarian bookseller, however, appeared to have seen and heard nothing, neither misnomer nor the sight of his patron McGill's scandalous behaviour. He had come here to read; and even Jasmine's cooing and long-winded refusal of a Bloody Mary followed by the mock-reluctant acceptance of the drink would not shake him from his determination.

Given Miss Bosanquet's uniquely maddening style, both self-congratulatory ('I can pride myself on being the possessor of a finely tuned consciousness second only, I may hazard, to that of the great Henry James') and making extraordinary claims of the psychic results of the Master's 'slow, deliberate voice' as it 'played over her', I have here taken the liberty of synopsizing her account of the visit to Lamb House (the first part at least: I was unaware then that there was more). As it is, the events described are obviously incredible – however, McGill it was who sent for the rare bookman from west London in order to entertain us over the festive season; and McGill it will be who suffers the scorn and disbelief of the audience collected here on a day of rapidly worsening weather: fog and probably snow are forecast. As their reactions, like the climate, were likely to become increasingly unfavourable, my ex-colleague Professor McGill was certain to absent himself from our little circle; and my sister-in-law would no longer be the recipient of his inappropriate advances. Together we would go in search of Lou, who must, I feared, be suffering from some sudden reminder of her father's recent demise – or possibly, as her pallor betokened yesterday, she did, unlike the ludicrous suffragette-cum-spiritualist Theodora Bosanquet, actually convince herself – poor Lou – that she had seen her father's ghost.

As I rose to my feet, eyes still firmly fixed on the window seat and on dear Mary's flustered, embarrassed expression at the actions of McGill, a couple of women's voices rang out. Salome, my Prada-robed horror, spoke first, then Jasmine, who was fast gathering a status only just below Salome in the hatred stakes. 'Can she explain how she gets these messages from the Other Side?' followed by Jasmine's announcement that a fictionalized biography of Henry James, with Miles and Flora as the children he had always longed to have – 'Can we discuss a Channel Four programme now planned?' – was aired raucously.

I did my best. Miss Bosanquet received her instructions from the Master by means of a machine not so dissimilar to her famous Remington, an Ouija board. (At this, Jasmine insisted on opening her 'Jane!' paper, but our hostess demanded patience, while Stephen from Bell Street simply stood on his dais and looked as if he had forgotten entirely how to move.)

I explained as best I could how 'planchette', as this form of communication with the spirit world is known, actually works – if one can put it that way, of course. The letters are arranged on a flat surface, an 'arm' of wood swings round and points to them, forming sentences that are answers to the players' requests.

'And what did Miss Bosanquet want to know?' demanded Salome. (Whether she expected a quick, efficient guide to shop-opening times one can barely surmise.)

So here we discovered the truth; and, despite all my pleas, there was no halting McGill's plan. He had only to begin, 'Henry James, according to Miss Bosanquet, dictated several novels in the decades after his death . . .' for the whole room, with its trembling Water-ford glass chandelier, its highly polished mahogany tables that reflected the excited faces of the listeners and the Persian carpets which each, in time-honoured country-house tradition, supported the slumbering figure of a Labrador or German Shepherd, to become as quiet as a nursery finally preparing for bedtime.

'He instructed Miss Bosanquet to go to Lamb House and find his one unfinished story,' McGill said in a voice intended to thrill an after-dinner audience.

When the cries of excitement had died down, all eyes turned to Stephen – and at last, driven by the hunger for stories, the promise of suspension of dis-belief maybe, the sheer need to believe that a great writer has a hidden manuscript he wishes to share, the room grew dark in the early winter afternoon and the words fell as softly and unobtrusively as the snow.

PART III

MISS BOSANQUET

I remember only the light in an empty shuttered room in the house on the hill, the house with its swath of cobbles and proudly closed garden gate – a light I can swear I had never seen before: blue or *bluish* I suppose you could call it, a light that did not belong here, in the watery world of Sandwich or Rye. I had never seen it before – yet I had heard it described, this extra-terrestrial glow, by those who had died and come back: it was the light at the end of the tunnel, the light for ghosts as they go stealthily from room to room in places where once they had known life.

This must explain why I stood still, rooted to the spot as one might say. Yet what was I waiting for, after all? Russell Noakes, or at least his outer carapace, had vanished entirely. The room was miserably cold. I had no inkling of where to go next – or what I must find. I had to bring back *something*, I knew – but what? An unfinished story? The Master's instructions had been erratic on that airless morning in July: I could barely understand what – or whom – I must seek out. And I knew myself to be alone – more alone than I had ever been, even on days in the past when the Master had gone to Brighton or Hove or visited his neighbours in the downs above Firle. The lack of the important object I must retrieve from Lamb House grew as I shrank inside myself to the size of a small child. I knew myself on the edge of letting down the greatest genius two centuries had known or will ever know. Henry James had left a valuable memento of his fine dictating days here. He needed and wanted it now; it would complete his life, his record, his tally of the finest works ever written on either side of the Atlantic.

As I stood, by now nearer the long windows in the panelled room, I saw a shutter had been drawn back, as if by a hand uncertain whether the interior of the famous house should remain hidden from the human gaze or be exposed to the fullness of day. And as I approached the old flaky wood of the shutter I remembered a woman, young, splendidly aware of her colonial upbringing, quietly assured of her married future – and I saw my predecessor Mary Weld as her image burned for a few seconds before me. She had gone – no, there was no repeat of the diminutive house servant's comparatively lengthy visit to the once-gracious building – she had disappeared even in memory before I could ascertain either direction or intention on her part. But, vaguely, I suspected the chimney-piece to be my goal: I thought I saw a small door in the panelling right up next to it – and there, if you can skip the intervening moments while I heard the sound of my own footsteps as they dragged across the parquet to the tall marble mantelpiece and the (uncleaned) grate, dull and black and littered with the ashes of the last occupant's duration here – I arrived and found my fingernails could slip into a join between faded wallpaper and panel on the wall. I pulled – then pushed. It swung open, and I went in.

A small room – more of what the French would call a *cabinet* – lay before me. There was a meanly proportioned window – it was as if, I remember thinking, whoever had fitted this secret chamber behind the gloriously proportioned Green Room had considered any incoming light to be unnecessary for its purposes and so had skimped on both glass and design. The room *did* look out, it was true, but on an interior courtyard, the kind of yard that has no place in today's domestic arrangements, where clothes are hung to dry or where possibly, as an archway led directly out from the courtyard to the back drive of the house, horses were brought in and washed down. All very Jane Austen, you might say (she is an author on whom the Master has written, and I am in total agreement with him as to her considerable abilities) – but the world of *Persuasion* or *Pride and Prejudice* was far removed on that strange day from the neglected and unwelcoming Lamb House. There was – how can I describe it? – a raw, almost toxic feeling to the tiny room, but then, as I must confess it took me some time to realize, my sight was not the only sense affected when I pushed open the swinging panel and walked in.

Paint! I was so assaulted by the strength of the smell (and, I asked myself later, how did I *know* the colour of the paint to be white when neither can nor brush was visible?) – I was so *floored* by its almost living presence that I ran to the tiny window to lift the sill and lean out into the courtyard in a desperate quest for air.

As I went, my skirt, skimpy as it was (we were still in an age of wartime clothing coupons), brushed against the one piece of furniture in what I shall refer to as a store room, for it was nothing more. A box – a chest, I suppose you could call it – stood directly under the unopenable window. A key lay on the lid of the box, and it was this that I had shaken from its place to the floor. Owing to the exiguous proportions of the hidey-hole I was forced to kneel to retrieve it – for I knew I must unlock the box and find my way back, close to suffocation as I already was, into the house where I had once transcribed the works of the Master. I can swear with a hand on my heart that I have never known the terror and sense of helplessness caused by the smell of paint in an unaired room. I wondered, I admit, if I was in the process of losing my sanity.

The key, after three fumbling attempts, fitted the lock of the chest. I had hardly the courage to look down at its meagre contents – but a glimpse afforded only a photograph of a woman in Edwardian bustle standing in this tiny room, holding a collection of papers. She wore an enigmatic smile. Next to her stood my much-respected late employer Henry James. He also held a bundle of papers; but his look, as he gazed at his typist, the one woman in whom he confided all his secrets, was far from enigmatic or contented. His look was one of pure horror, extreme anxiety. I scrabbled beneath the photograph and pulled out a sheaf of papers, type-written and yellowing with age.

This is all I remember before the smell of the paint finally overcame me.

When I was next conscious I saw a man in gardening clothes who knelt by me in the Green Room – he must have dragged me in there and then gone for help, for a charwoman with her head turbaned like all working women in the 1940s and 1950s was trying to encourage me to sip from a mug of scalding tea.

A taxi was called from an ancient black telephone in the hall of Lamb House. It was a long wait, but the front door was open, the weather had changed and a gusty wind accompanied by a spatter of rain revived me.

On the train journey back to London I opened the sheaf of papers I had taken from the chest – the same papers as those held, as if in some game of cat and mouse, by the great writer and his secretary. I began to read – and it was only when we arrived at Victoria and the pages remaining were no more than a handful that I reluctantly made my way out and down the platform to find a cab that would bring me home.

God will give me strength in my pursuit of the truth.

PROFESSOR JAN
SUNDERLAND

If I were to pen a sketch of that evening at the Media
Manor, the minutes succeeding Miss Bosanquet's
arrival on the station platform, secret missive in hand
(has it been understood, I wonder, that a secretary may
originally have been regarded as a *secret-keeper*? I shall
instruct my students to discuss), I would dwell on the
short period during which our secondhand bookman
paused and was handed a glass of water by our effusive
hostess – for it demonstrated clearly the change in
priorities amongst the listeners. Douglas McGill's hand,
my first port of call when it came to looking around the
room, had slid away from my sister-in-law altogether.
A gold fountain pen now sat authoritatively between
his first and second fingers. The Professor had been
joined by the man I knew only as 'Mike'; the taciturn
dominie of Creative Writing. McGill was speaking in a
low voice, but I heard him excitedly exclaim that Miss
Bosanquet's deposition – along with something he
referred to as 'the fragment' – had famously disappeared
some years ago, and if it had not been for the sharp eye
of the bookseller from Bell Street it might have stayed
'lost' for many years to come. 'A disgrace for Harvard,'

McGill concluded, while looking over at me in quiet triumph: did I not know about the 'fragment' that had been lost or stolen?

Meanwhile, our friend from Paddington cleared his throat once more and asked if he should continue his reading.

'Let's just go straight on,' insisted my old foe Salome. I suspected the sartorial show-off to have slipped upstairs during the recent reading to change into her Vivien Westwood 'ironic parody' of a post-feminist prostitute: this, at least, I had overheard her whisper loudly as her intention to the Mistress of Ceremonies. But, owing to a bad memory and very little dress sense. I had no way of comparing and parsing the young woman's outfits. Not for the first time I wished Mary, ensconced on the window seat with a dreamy expression on her face – perhaps she missed McGill's hand: but I decided, as my students would say, not to go there – I wished my sister-in-law would look just once in my direction. Questions on how to proceed could then be analysed: as it was, I had no idea whether the demand that Stephen read straight on came from a genuine follower of Henry James or a disciple of Prada; and I had always imagined the latter.

So, as I knew only one way to attract the attention of the mother of my niece Lou, I looked quickly around the room before attempting to pronounce on the matter. The Jane Eyre student was still in place at the table, scribbling and looking up from time to time as if to refresh her impressions of the people in the much-reduced audience. She saw – I saw her seeing – Doug McGill, Mike and my sister-in-law Mary on the window seat in the bay window. Her gaze swept over Salome, who had taken to shooting her arm up in the air to command attention like a junior-school pupil; and she saw, of course, the host and hostess, who were now mixing bullshots in a small high-tech pantry off the drawing-room.

I regret it took some time for the absence of Jasmine to sink in. She was a pleasant enough little woman, I would be the first to allow – but she was eminently forgettable. The other absentee was Lou – Lou, the expert on all things Jamesian: I was eager to find her and hear her opinion on Miss Bosanquet's memoir.

❖ ❖

I left the dining-room slightly surprised, I must own, to receive no questioning glances, no inquisitive eye contact from the media celebrity hosts; I must be of little importance to them, I was unable to resist concluding. For there may be a film 'in development' or a series of detective television episodes with Henry James as a pudgy sleuth – but the day of the book, the true study of the 'real right thing', is definitely over. Plot has replaced talent, sense of an ending, whatever you like to call it. In this 21st-century bogus Edwardian mansion the novels of James Joyce or Henry Green would be considered 'unacceptable' and consigned to the bin.

These gloomy thoughts got me as far as the foot of the ornamental staircase leading upwards to the bedroom floor. Lou must be there – out of sorts or suffering from the new influenza which has graced us with a visit this year. Why her mother, still marooned by the sight of McGill, has not gone in search of her I cannot imagine; but I, her guardian and encourager since the death of her father, guiding her in a casual but earnestly intentioned way through the maze of Maisie and into the finer shadings of the mind of the dying heroine Millie Theale, will keep an avuncular eye on her for as long as it is necessary. In the event – God forbid! – that Mary remarries (not McGill, I almost spoke aloud in my prayer for the continuing status of my sister-in-law as a widow; please not McGill) it will be to me that poor Lou will turn; and I will not let her down or disappoint her.

The wide cedar-banistered staircase bore me up rapidly; and I was at the entrance to the long passage from which my own room and many others lead off before I had stopped my sad reflections of the state of the novel, its decline and the splendours of James's melodramatic tales, emerging as they do from a mass of adoring sentences and triumphant in their capture of both meaning and morality.

I was walking along the runner – Persian, ugly, just the kind of carpet that would portray no figure, utterly bland, probably imitation, like the work of all the aspiring 'novelists' of today – when I felt myself gripped just above the elbow. My wrist was grasped and for a few seconds held captive by a hand that, even as I shrank back from the encounter, insinuated itself further along the cuff of my shirt. It was a hand but a strange hand, I realized with growing horror, with perhaps two or more fingers missing. A smooth expanse of skin caused by their absence accounted for a weakness in the grip.

The corridor appeared to have grown very dark, in those seconds of my attack – as I was later to consider this event, for it was certainly no friendly approach; and why or how I convinced myself that the sudden increase of gloom in the passageway was my reason for failing to see my assailant I simply do not know.

I know only that a very faint tang accompanied the feel of the soft skin and barely palpable stumps of the ruffian on the stairs (it was my sole encounter to date with death, which accounts for the literary allusions and fancy language that presented themselves to me on this strange occasion) and I feared the loss of my sanity, for surely I had been obsessing about McGill's hand – was I jealous, did I desire poor Mary, was I an incestuous Claudius to her Gertrude? The tang, the trace of a smell, grew stronger as I stumbled towards the door which I knew would lead to Lou's room. Paint; oil paint – it faded almost as soon as it was recognized – then grew a little stronger as I grabbed the doorknob and went in. The hand – as if it had led me to my destination – slipped out of mine and disappeared.

Lou was lying in a four-poster bed, a phoney Jacobean four-poster it was, with curtains of some kind of chintz drawn back on both sides.

A woman stood near the fireplace. A fine log fire crackled behind her. The woman had the stooping stance of a Cranach nude, the slight air of apology, the fuzz of floating hair. At first, I confess, it was harder to put a name to her than it had been to identify the smell of fresh paint. But then – for she knew me, it seemed: she walked a few steps towards me and then stood still – it came back, her first name at least. Jasmine, wife of the unbearable Mike. I managed to blurt out a greeting.

Lou just lay there. One anguished look and I saw she was paler than ever, with dark circles that looked as if they had been crudely crayoned under her eyes.

MISS BOSANQUET

Now I am safely in my flat in Old Chelsea, close to the watery Thames-scapes of Turner and Whistler and the other Theodore, Roussel, I am able to report on the pages found in a seaman's chest in what must have been, in those infinitely more gracious days, a Georgian powder room at Lamb House.

I feel immensely proud, I must confess, to have been entrusted with the task of encouraging the Master to finish the story – the only tale, in all his many productive years, which he failed to complete.

My predecessor Mary Weld had thoughtfully tucked into the long envelope her diary entries for the dates – all in July 1902 – when Henry James battled most manfully with *The Beautiful Child*, as his work in progress was named. A note in his dear, clear hand informs us of the eccentric *provenance* of the *conte*. He had been given the idea by a friend, Paul Bourget, of a story about a couple who wanted – or who *had wanted* – a child; who were aware that they could never have one now; and who approached a society painter and asked him to paint an imaginary child for them.

Oh, this material was perfect for the Master! As I

read I was enchanted as always by the rich wit, the ironies and paradoxes, of a piece of writing accomplished at the height of his powers. The artist selected for the task of 'bringing to life' a phantom offspring was also perfectly delineated: a touch obsequious, true, but a *real* artist, Hugh Merrow could have sprung from the pen of only one author, an author of genius: Henry James.

At first I did not spend time in wondering why this tale, unlike all the long, exhausting novels (to write, of course I mean, not to read: I have no sympathy for those who claim to have been excessively tried by the late novels, *The Wings of the Dove*, *The Ambassadors* or *The Golden Bowl*). But as I read on I did see that *The Beautiful Child*, clearly considered worthy of an effort as great as any other in his *œuvre* (for a tale, at least), demanded some explanation for its state of pre-adolescent immaturity. Why could the Master, so gifted when it came to children (fictional, naturally: it was always impossible to see Henry James as a father), be so totally at a loss when it came to solving the problem posed by *The Beautiful Child*? And what was this problem? Why, it was hardly a problem at all, and in any case it was one that had been settled easily in many instances, that is, the determining of the sex of the child to be portrayed. The Nandas, the Maisies, the Daisys – I knew them all, and it had not occurred to me once that their gender had been arrived at with difficulty: that the girls could have been conceived as boys and vice versa, and they had all been in a Middlesex of the mind until the final decision was taken. Sometimes, it was true, the author had plumped for one of each – the most famous example being Miles and Flora in *The Turn of the Screw*. But there were reasons for this: a boy goes away to school, and Miles's profanity, never given in detail, took place when he was a boarder. Flora, the girl, suffers her terrors in the supposed safety of the home.

I shall continue here with the incomplete story itself. I have retrieved it for the Master; and, as soon as he hears the click of my Remington he will know that this long-forgotten work will be legible and ready for his keen perusal. (I wish to make no comment on the level of typing skills demonstrated by my predecessor, Miss Weld: suffice it to say that typos, as they are known in our crude age of faceless typists in pools overseen by monstrous bosses – how far from dear Miss Petheridge's Secretarial Bureau! – appear to have been her speciality.) Had the story not lain buried all this time, to be rescued half a century later by one such as myself, the priceless words of the Master would have remained mangled and misspelt: an unthinkable fate for a justly celebrated writer, a man whose every word has been weighed and deliberated. One wonders, to let Mary Weld off the hook just a little, what exactly *was* going on in the summer of 1902? Doubtless the heat was partly responsible for the frequent errors – but Miss Weld enjoyed a colonial upbringing: surely the month of July in Sussex cannot have affected her work so drastically?

❖ ❖

My heart beats as I go over to the Remington, my haunted machine, my conduit to what I have described to my late employer as the Outernet, the great web beyond the stars where the dead can communicate with the living. The Master will respond via the Ouija board, as always: when I have typed the unfinished tale and placed it on my (and his) beloved typewriter he will instruct me to prepare for dictation.

Then I will begin.

But even as I assume the careful listening stance of a devoted amanuensis, something tells me I may rebel and round off the story myself.

Yet such heresy is unthinkable, even after fifty years. I will, as ever, take down the words of the Master; and I shall obey his instructions to the letter, as he would of course anticipate from his devoted secretary, Theodora Bosanquet.

PROFESSOR JAN
SUNDERLAND

'Isn't it time we went to Lamb House? I'm bored.' The tall young woman kicked her horribly wedge-heeled platform numbers up in the air while remaining seated, a feat I attributed to the pelvic-floor exercises one had overheard her discussing with the Sales Babes – as I had christened the absent girls from God-knows-where. 'I mean, there's been no trace of a ghost unless you count a stupid dwarf who is probably still alive and drawing his pension! What is the point of this Bosanquet woman anyway? She's fainting all over the place when all she has to do is find a half-baked Henry James story. Obviously, the "Master" knew it was no good, so he abandoned it. Worse things have happened at sea!'

Part of me couldn't help admiring Miss Harrods Couture for not giving a damn if she offended our hostess (evidently she had, for a throat-clearing, watch-consulting and rattling of ice cubes in readiness for further bullshots became suddenly loud) – but I also felt a moment of pride when my Jane Eyre student spoke up and said she didn't think this was the right time for a visit to the house up the steep hill in Rye.

'We need to know that story' came in her – slightly maddening – quiet voice. I wasn't even sure whether Salome had heard her. But I had hardly looked over at the bay window with its distinctly Turneresque light effects between bouts of all-obliterating snow – with another soft voice coming in agreement – when it became clear that my sister-in-law was still there on the window seat. The curtain that had previously shielded Lou from the gaze of the Armani army now virtually concealed all of her mother. Of Doug McGill there was no sign.

'It is essential that we understand the story Henry James was trying to write,' Mary was saying, as Salome raised her dramatically blackened eyebrows and muttered disagreement, if I picked up her half-Estuary, half-ladies'-finishing-school accent accurately.

'There's not too much to understand' came the voice of a man as he emerged from the pantry, cocktail shaker in hand. 'James was unable to crack the problem of the central couple's economic situation. He had *The Wings of the Dove* in mind, where a corrupt journalist fakes love for an heiress in order to set up his girlfriend in the style to which she has become accustomed . . .'

'He was a paedophile,' Salome barked back at the now-recognizable Mike who, visibly affected by the contents of the shaker, swayed over to the window seat and lowered himself down next to Mary. 'He'd be in gaol today. He was lucky to get away with it then. *The Child . . . The Beautiful Child* – for Christ's sake, what does that point to except a lascivious old man jerking off on a hot summer day . . . No wonder he gave it all up in July! Or maybe the typist, poor bitch, Theodora . . .'

'Mary Weld took dictation from James in 1902 and continued to do so for a further five years,' my almost inaudible student put in doggedly.

'Well, I'm going anyway,' Salome announced. And, with a toss of her head one couldn't help admiring – this was no Anna Karenina, no Tess of the d'Urbervilles, surely more of a Lucrezia Borgia – she swung down from the table she had taken since the mass emigration of the M&S bargain-basement-hunters and clattered out of the room.

'But the snow, the snow,' our media hospitality provider shouted after her in exasperation. 'Please, please . . .'

We all heard the front door, a particularly unconvincing ersatz mahogany one complete with fake old brass knocker, as it crunched shut behind her. Only Mike's slurred tones rose above the wall of silence and surprise that followed Salome's departure; and if I was the sole occupant of the dining-room to gaze in even greater amazement at the Manchester Marxist's next pronouncement then I feel sure that my degree of shock was high enough to compensate for the lack of interest of any of the others gathered there.

'What did Mr and Mrs Archdean offer the artist Merrow for his portrait of the imaginary child? James did not specify. Here we find an unsuccessful attempt to write a petit-bourgeois tale where the fascination the artist clearly feels for the future mother of the not-yet-depicted child replaces the harsh realities of the artist's life at the beginning of the twentieth century. Who here knows what the income of, say, John Singer Sargent was at that time? I can tell you . . .'

Before Mike could finish his sentence I had made rapidly for the door. In the hall I saw McGill as he hurried to resume his position on the window seat.

But for once I didn't care. For the scene I had so recently left – Lou's room and her silent, exhausted shake of the head when I pressed her to tell me how she was – still mystified and baffled me. As did Jasmine, wife of Mike, as she stood by the fireplace, head low, while appearing to look right through me when I attempted to draw her into a conversation. 'Of course we have met,' she had said at last, after shooting, as I saw, a protective angry glance at the pale figure in the four-poster. And at last, but still hesitatingly, she held out her hand to me – in a quaint, old-fashioned way.

'Isabel Archdean,' this mysterious visitor to Lou had then introduced herself. 'Have you come with a message from Mr Merrow? When can he begin the portrait?'

❖ ❖

Now I am sitting as far from the secondhand book-dealer as I can get – on the window seat and unpleasantly close to both McGill and the man I had known as 'Mike'. A silence fell that was more demanding of attention than before – only a flurry of snow coming down the chimney brought a little gasp of fear from my poor Jane Eyre.

'The Beautiful Child,' the wispy little bibliophile on the raised stool read out. And so, finally, he began.

THE BEAUTIFUL CHILD – AN UNFINISHED STORY BY HENRY JAMES

*I*T WAS ONLY for a moment that Merrow failed to place them, aware as he was, as soon as they were introduced, of having already seen them. That was all they at first showed, except that they were shy, agitated, almost frightened: they had been present to him, and within a few days, though unwittingly, in some connection that had made them interesting. He had recovered the connection even before the lady spoke – spoke, he could see, out of the depths of their diffidence and making the effort, he could also see, that the woman, in the delicate case, is always left by the man to make. 'We admire so very much your portrait at the Academy – the one of the beautiful little boy. We've had no one to introduce us to you, but we thought you would perhaps just let us call. We've – a – been wondering. We were so struck.'

'We were most awfully struck,' said the young husband, who was as 'nice-looking' in his way as she in hers – and indeed their ways were much the same. He gained confidence from his wife's attack.

'Oh, I'm sure I'm happy to see you. You've – a – been wondering?' Yet he hardly liked, Hugh Merrow, to take the words out of their mouths. 'Struck' he had seen they were, struck with his picture of happy little Reggie Blyth, six years old, erect in a sailor-suit, so struck that their attitude in front of it, three days before, was what had made him remember them – he having been really as much impressed with it as they, poor dears, had been with his work. He had gone back to the exhibition, just open, to look at a couple of things by friends to which he had apparently not done justice on varnishing day or at the private view, admonished thereto by an apparent perception of the failure in the friends themselves, whom he had since met and to whom, with an amenity altogether characteristic of him, he wished to make it up. Moving through the rooms on his way out he had not denied himself the pleasure, nor avoided the imprudence, of passing within eyeshot of his own principal performance, partly for the joy of again seeing himself so luckily hung. If either of the two friends to whom he wished to make it up had chanced to be there with a different motive – they were hung so much worse – they might easily have had their revenge by accusing him of hovering greedily where he could catch compliments. They would indeed have been justified in the sense that he had, indubitably, slackened pace at the sight of the pleasant – oh, the peerless! – young couple who were so evidently lost in admiration. Their attention had affected him, at a glance, as so serious and so sweet that instinctively, with the artist's well-known 'need' of appreciation, he had treated himself to the bare opportunity of picking up some word that would further express it. And he had been to that extent repaid that a remarkable expression, on the young woman's lips, had reached his ear. 'Oh, it kills me!' – that was what she had strangely sighed: yet without turning off and rather as if she like to be killed. Merrow had himself turned off – he had got rather more than he wanted. He winced for compunction, as if he had pushed too far, and it served him right that what she had said needn't in the least have been a tribute to the painter. He guessed, in fact, on the spot the situation: it was a case of a young husband and a young wife deprived by death of a little boy of whom Reggie Blyth, extraordinarily handsome, blooming with life and promise – under a master-hand certainly – too poignantly reminded them. Reggie, clearly, resembled their child, brought him back, opened their wound; in spite of which they were still fascinated – they had seemed fairly to devour him. But their interest had been in him, not in Hugh Merrow: so that on their thus reappearing their proper motive immediately presented itself. What they had been 'wondering', as the wife said, was, inevitably, whether they mightn't perhaps persuade him to paint their little dead boy. They would have photographs, perhaps some other portrait, some domestic drawing, or even some fatuous baby bust, and their appeal to him – from which it was natural they should hang back – would be on behalf of these objects and of such suggestions and contributes as they might otherwise make.

That, as I say, had quickly come to him – with the one contradictory note indeed that mourning was not their wear; whereby the death of the child would not have been recent. He saw it all, at any rate – and partly from habit, for he had been approached repeatedly for a like purpose, such being the penalty of a signal gift: but he saw it disappointedly as he had seen it before and the qualification of his welcome to the errand of these visitors cost him the greater effort as the visitors themselves were unmistakeably amiable. They were visibly such a pair as would always be spoken of in the same way – 'Oh yes, the young Archdeans; charming people.' He was in possession of their name through the presentation of their card before their entrance. They were charming people because in the first place they could feel – which was an aptitude one seemed, in the world, to encounter less and less; and because in the second, as husband and wife, they felt so together – were so touchingly, so prettily, as he might call it, united in their impulse. The tall young man, all shapely straightness of feature and limb, erectness that was not stiffness, with his simple but sensitive face, his rich colour, his pleasant clothes, his lapse of assurance, had been as much taken by their idea, Merrow knew, as the bereaved mother herself, whose type, equally fortunate, equally a thing of achieved fineness, though not on the present occasion a thing of better balance, added the light that made the painter inwardly exclaim as he read their story and looked from one to the other, 'What a beautiful child it must have been!' That stuck out for him, awake as he was to the charm of beauty, harmony, felicity, of everything that made for 'race' – what beautiful children they ought to have! He had seen so many of the mismatched and misbegotten that his eyes rested with a sudden surrender on this appearance of forces – if they could be called forces. He was in fact so held that while Mrs Archdean continued to explain, he quite lost, for the instant, the sense of her words. He was thinking that she was ever so delicately and dimly pretty, that her mouth was as sweet as her eyes, and her nose as handsome as her hair; and he was thinking other things besides. They were charming people partly because happy conditions had produced them, easily, goodly, generous English conditions, current London plenitudes, such as would operate, in turn, by the fact of their own happiness, which couldn't fail to be always decorative, always at least enhancing to the general scene, by mere casual presence.

But what distinguished them for Merrow, of a truth, still more than these comparatively commonplace elements of good luck and good humour, was the way they made him think of them as above all exquisitely at one with each other. He was single, he was, behind everything, lonely, and it had been given him so little to taste of any joy of perfect union, that he was, as to many matters, not even at one with himself. The joy of perfect union, nevertheless, had hovered before him as a dream – in consequence of which he was now insidiously moved by this presentation of a case of it. These handsome, tender, bereaved young persons were acting in entire concert. They had plenty of pleasures, but none would be so great for them as for him to attempt what they proposed. The wife, moreover, would care for it in the measure in which it would touch the husband; the husband would care for it in the measure in which it would touch the wife. This it was that made them beautiful, and from this it was that his disturbing thought sprang. Even as Mrs Archdean proceeded, helplessly, with her errand, he said to himself that it was them he should like to paint, and to paint intensely together. He already saw how he should express it in the truth that, in their world where so much had been loosened, they were intensely together. It was an association free from worldly, from vulgar dis-agreements. So at least our friend had judged it till it threw out a surprise for him. He found himself presently with something else to think of; having meanwhile met the enquiry of his visitors as nearly half way as was permitted by his small eagerness to work from photographs and conversations.

'It's not a little boy we should like – or at least I should,' said Mrs Archdean. 'It's a little girl.'

Her husband, at this, as Hugh looked vague, laughed out his awkwardness. 'We don't, we should tell you, feel quite the same about it. My own idea's the boy – all the more after seeing how you do them. But of course it's for you to say.' Our young man was amused, but he tried not to show it. 'Which would you had rather have?'

'Which do you think you could do best?' said Mrs Archdean.

He met her eyes, and he was afterwards to remember that what he had then seen in them was the very

— 74 —

beginning, the first faint glimmer – yet with a golden light, however dim – of a relation. She intensely appealed to him; she privately approached him; she attempted an understanding with him apart from her husband – and this though her affection for her husband was complete. Of course, moreover, it was open to that personage to attempt another understanding. All this was much for Hugh to see in a few seconds; but he had not painted portraits ten years for nothing. 'And then, you've both a boy and a girl?'

'No – unfortunately not,' said Captain Archdean with a queer face.

'Oh, you've had the grief of losing them?' Merrow considerately suggested.

It produced, oddly, a silence, as if each of his companions waited for the other to speak. It was the wife again who had to clear it up. 'We have no children. We've never had any.'

'Oh!' said her host in vagueness.

'That's our bad case' – and Captain Archdean, for relief, still treated it with a measure of gaiety. 'We should have liked awfully to. But here we are.'

'Do you mean – a – ? ' But Hugh could scarce imagine what they meant.

'We shall never have any,' the young wife went on. 'We've hoped, we've waited. But now we're sure.'

'Oh!' said Hugh Merrow again.

'From the moment we came we had to tell you all this, and perhaps you'll only think us ridiculous. But we've talked it over long – it has taken all our courage. We gained a great deal – so you see it's partly your own doing – from the sight of your child.'

She had so sounded her possessive that Merrow was for the moment at a loss. 'Mine? Ah,' he said cheeringly, 'if I could only have one as well!'

'I mean the one at the Academy – the dear little sailor-man. You can have as many as you like – when you can paint them that way!'

'Ah, I don't paint them for myself,' our young man laughed. 'I paint them – with a great deal of difficulty, and not always all as I want – for others.'

'That's just it,' Captain Archdean observed more lucidly than before. 'We're just such a pair of others – only we shouldn't make you any sort of difficulty. Not any,' he added with a spasm of earnestness that showed Merrow both what he meant and how he felt. His desire was so great that it overcame his reluctance to mention the subject of price. He was ready to pay the highest the artist could be conceived as asking. 'All we want is that he should be such a one as we might have had.'

'Oh, better than that,' the young woman interposed. 'We might have had one with some blot, some defect, some affliction. We want her perfect – without a flaw. Your little boy' – and she again, for her host, uncontrollably intensified the pronoun – 'is the absolute ideal for everything.'

'So that to make ours the same,' said her husband. 'Mr Merrow will have to make him a boy.'

She looked again at the painter. 'I think you'll have to tell us first that we don't appear to you crazy.'

Merrow, while he, as before, met her look, found himself aware of a drop of his first disappointment. There was something in her that made – and made, in effect, quite insistently – for a relation; that positively forced it on him as, for his own part, a charity or an act of good manners. And it made the difference that he didn't much care if they were crazy or not, or even if he himself were. Their funny errand had begun to appeal to him, but it would be part of the fun that they should fully state their case. Merrow desired this, moreover, in no spirit of derision; he already saw that, pleasant as they were, there was no fun; for anyone concerned in the transaction would be obstreperous. 'What exactly is it then that you ask of me?'

'Well, absurd as it may seem, to give us what we're not so happy as to have otherwise, to create for us a sort of imitation of the little source of pleasure of which we're deprived. That – as you know you may do it – will be something.'

Merrow considered. 'Haven't you thought of adoption?'

Captain Archdean now promptly answered. 'Very much. We've looked at a hundred children. But they won't do.'

'They're not it,' said his wife.

'They're not him,' he explained.

'They're not her,' she continued. 'You see, we know what we would like.'

'Oh, but you don't quite seem to!' Merrow laughed. 'Is it a boy or a girl?'

'Which would you rather do?' Mrs Archdean enquired.

'Which would most naturally come to you, for ease, for reality?'

'Ah, reality!' Merrow good-humouredly groaned. 'Reality's hard to arrive at with so little to go upon. You offer me, you see, no data, no documents. It's worse even than if she were dead.'

'Oh, thank God she's not dead!' Mrs Archdean oddly exclaimed. 'We give you a free hand, but we trust you.'

Again Merrow paused. 'Have you tried anyone else?'

She looked about the room, at studies, heads, figures placed, a little at random, on the walls, and at two or three things on easels, started, unfinished, but taking more or less the form of life. One of these last was, as happened, another portrait of a child, precisely of a little girl, pretty and interested, eminently paintable, in whom our young man had found an inspiration. The thing but foreshadowed his intention, yet the essence of the face seemed the more to look out from it; and Mrs Archdean, who had approached it, turned from it, after a long gaze, to answer. 'No – it's something we've never imagined till now.'

'Not,' said her husband, 'till we had seen your little Reggie. It all comes from that – he put it into our heads. It came to us – to both of us at the same moment – that if you could do him you could do what we want.' The poor gentleman, making every concession for the absurd sound of their story, yet the more assured, or the more indifferent for having broken, as he evidently felt, an inordinate amount of ice, paused again, pressingly, and again struck out. 'It's the idea, you see, of something that would live with us. He'll be there – he'll be in the house. It won't be as it is now.'

'With nothing!' the young mother, as she wished to be, strangely sighed.

'When we look up we shall seem him,' her companion said. 'And when we talk we shall mention him. He'll have his name.'

'Oh, he'll have everything!' – Mrs Archdean repeated her murmur. 'Your little boy,' she went on, 'has everything. How,' she asked, 'could you part with him?'

'Oh,' said Merrow, 'I've lost so many that I'm used to it.'

She looked at him as if studying in his face the signs – deep and delicate as they would be – of so much experience. 'And you can have as many more as you like.'

Merrow didn't deny it; he was thinking of something else. 'Have you seen little Reggie himself?'

'Oh dear, no!'

'We don't want to,' Captain Archdean explained. 'We wouldn't for the world.' He had arrived at stating the facts of their odd attitude very much as a patient consulting a doctor enumerates aches and pains.

And his wife added her touch. 'We don't like children – that is, other people's. We can't bear them – when they're beautiful. They make us too unhappy. It's only when they're not nice that we can look at them. Yours is the only nice one we've for a long time been able to think of. It's something in the way you've done him.' With which she looked again at the little girl on the easel. 'You're doing it again – it's something in yourself. That's what we felt.' She had said all, and she wound up with an intimate glance at her husband. 'There you have us.'

And Merrow felt indeed that he did; he was in possession; he knew, about their charming caprice, all that was to be known, though perhaps not quite whether the drollery or the poetry of it were what most touched him. It was almost puerile, yet it was rather noble. 'Of course,' he presently said, 'I feel the beauty and the rarity of your idea. It's highly original – it quite takes hold of me.'

'It isn't that we don't see it ourselves as wildly fantastic!' one of them hastened to concede; to which he found himself replying, with a sound of attenuation, that this was not necessarily against it. But it was, just then, by a word of the young wife's that he was most arrested. 'The worse we shall have done will be after all but to make you refuse.'

'And what will you do if I refuse?'

'Well, we shan't go to anyone else.'

'We shall go on as we have done,' said Captain Archdean with a slight dryness of decency.

'Oh well,' Merrow answered, more and more determined; he was conscious, in the sense of good humour, of an indulgence as whimsical even as their own proposal – 'oh well, I don't want you to take me as stupidly unaccommodating, as having too little imagination, even if you yourselves have perhaps too much. It's just the intrinsic difficulty that makes me hesitate. It's the question of doing a thing so much in the air. There's such a drawback as having too free a hand. For little Reggie, you see, I had my model. He was exquisite, but he was definite – he lighted my steps. The question is what will light them in such a case as you propose. You know, as you say, what you want, but how exactly am I to know it?'

This enquiry, he could see, was not one that Captain Archdean could easily meet; and it was to be singular for him later on that he had entertained at the moment itself a small but sharp prevision, involving absolutely a slight degree of suspense, that their companion would, after an instant, be less at a loss. He really almost decided to let the matter depend on what she might say; according to which it depended with some intensity. He was not unaware that in spite of the scant response of the painter in him, who could but judge the invitation as to a wild-goose chase, he had been already moved, to rather a lively tune, by curiosity. It was as if something might come to him if he did consent, though what might come indeed might not be a thing that he himself should call a picture. Whatever it was to be, at any rate, it affected him at the end of another minute as having begun to come; for by that time Mrs Archdean had spoken, his suspense was relieved, his prevision was justified as to her not being so simple a person as her husband. 'Won't your steps really by lighted by your interest?'

He wondered. 'My interest in what, dear madam? In you and your husband?'

'Oh dear, no. In the artistic question itself – which we only suggest to you. In forming a conception which shall be, as you say of little Reggie, definite. In making it definite. In inventing, in finding, in doing – won't it be?

– what the artist does. I mean when he tries. For we do,' she added with a smile, 'want you to try hard.'

It was the same light note as her husband's some minutes before, a hint of great remuneration, should remuneration help the matter. But her smile corrected the slight impatience of the previous words and warranted Merrow's responding with the pleasantest pliancy. 'First catch your hare –! Do you mean I should be at liberty to reproduce some existing little person?'

The young woman, as with kindled hope, looked at him ever so gently. 'That's your affair. We should ask no questions.'

'We should only like the little person,' Captain Archdean intervened, 'to be somebody quite unknown to us and whom we should be likely never to see.'

His wife reassured him with a look. 'He'd change her, disguise her, improve her.' And she turned again to their host. 'You'd make her right. It's what we trust you for. We'd take her so, with our eyes closed, from your hands.'

Her face as she said this became somehow, for Hugh Merrow, more beautiful than before; and the impression had to do with his still more lending himself, even while he kept judging technically the vanity of the task. 'I should naturally have the resource of making her as much as possible like her supposed mother.'

'Oh,' Mrs Archdean returned with her eyes on her husband, 'I should wish her as much as possible like her supposed father. If that counts as a condition you must be merciful to it, for it's my only one.'

Captain Archdean faced the speakers in an attempt to

combine the air of confessed and cheerful eccentricity with the fact of something more inward, a real anxiety for the fate of the image he had projected, or perhaps, still more, his wife had; then he made a point that served as a refuge for his modesty. 'It's not a little girl, you know, who would naturally look like me.'

Merrow conscientiously demurred. 'I beg your pardon – there's nothing she might more easily do. But Mrs Archdean, I judge,' he continued, 'dreams of a little girl in your likeness, while you dream of a little boy in hers.'

'That's it,' the Captain genially granted. 'One sees little boys like their mother.'

'Well, the thing is so fundamental,' said our friend, 'that you really must settle it between you.'

The remark produced a pause, slightly awkward, to which Mrs Archdean, again a little impatiently, made an end. 'Oh, I could of course do with such a possession as little Reggie.'

'There it is!' her husband exclaimed. 'It's of that picture that one can't not think.'

'I see – yes,' Merrow returned. 'But I'm afraid I myself can't think of it much more. When once I've done a thing – !'

Captain Archdean looked at him harder. 'You prefer something different?'

Merrow waited a moment, during which their companion again spoke. 'Is it really quite impossible for you to decide?'

He still wondered. 'Why, you see you're both so handsome – !'

'Well then,' the Captain laughed. 'Make him resemble us both!"

'You'll at any rate really think of it?' said his wife. 'I mean, think of which will be best.'

Her fine young face quite terribly pleaded, and there was no use his pretending to ignore the fact of the recognition of feeling in her. He felt her to know him, to have seen him. He again answered her inwardly and for himself before speaking – and speaking differently – to her ear and to her husband's. He found himself trying to see in her what she must have been as a child, and he so far made it out that he held for a moment the vision of something too tenderly fair. Yes, he had painted children, but he had never painted the thing that – say at eight years old – she would have been. 'It will take much thought, but I'll give it all I can.'

'And about what will be the age – ?'

'Well, say about eight.'

This made them at once eager. 'Then you'll readily try?' They spoke in the same breath.

'I'll try my very hardest!'

They looked at each other in joy, too grateful even to speak. It was wonderful how he pleased them, and he felt that he liked it. If he could only keep it up!

PROFESSOR JAN SUNDERLAND

It would be hard to describe the silence that descended that day on the post-Lutyens 'country-house dining-room' nightmare which was to be our home until the end of the festivities – and I am in any case averse to descriptive writing (as was Thomas Hardy): my students are always surprised to be informed that none of the great Wessex novels contain any descriptions of the landscape at all – so I will say simply that the windows that once looked out on marshland and gentle snow-fall were now adorned with outer frames, of freezing snow and ice, giving one the impression of being trapped inside a particularly sickening set of Christmas cards.

But the silence – I must confess I missed my high-booted, mini-skirted foe at that moment of realization: the moment, that is, when it becomes clear that poor Hugh Merrow, the artist in the aborted story who hopes only too frantically that he will be able to 'keep it up', was clearly inspired by his own progenitor, Henry James. What the disappointed revellers in the media monstrosity would make of it all I could easily surmise, but Salome – the delightfully outspoken Salome – I needed her here to counteract the silence, which lay like cotton wool – or indeed like a further blanket of snow – all around us. And the fault lay entirely with myself, Professor Jan Sunderland: I, the Jamesian, the parser of his erotic verbs, the setter of this flat, tasteless quiz, for who by now, having listened to the self-absorbed, wispy-haired bookseller reading to us with quiet satisfaction, who could give a damn, now the promised fragment had been aired, what the sex of the couple's child would turn out to be? Boy/girl/hermaphrodite, what did it matter? We are over a century on from the drawing-room simpering and sniggering the tale would once have brought in its wake; now it seems merely to toll the death knell of the Master as he struggled to put in shape the New York edition of his work – and by no means necessarily improve the great novels and stories that had formed his lifetime struggle against the obvious, the trivial, the banal. Whatever the motives of this great writer may have been in deciding to call a halt to *The Beautiful Child*, we must respect – and indeed, we do respect – the writings of those impelled to try to understand the Master and to riddle out his secrets despite the triumph of his bonfire, which destroyed so many records of his private life.

No, Ms Cynthia Ozick, your essay 'Henry James's Unborn Child' is quite ludicrous in its claim that the choosing of an ideal offspring for the childless couple in the story brought James 'too close to the birth canal' and his abrupt cessation of the tale marked his refusal to be a mother. Tosh, indeed!

Meanwhile, I must give my thanks to my hostess – I have reviled her so far, I know – for seeing my predicament and, perhaps as only one who has been a television celebrity can do, changing the mood and encouraging guests to believe, however wrongly, that they are actually having a good time. It was when, looking around the room with her glassy blue-eyed stare, and chuckling behind a flashing smile – all this succeeded by a policewoman's frown as a new game show was announced and prizes were offered 'up to ten thousand pounds! Tonight!' – that I saw the door of the little high-tech pantry open behind her and a hand poke forward: a child's hand, I thought, as it barely reached our media lady's sequinned midriff. It held an envelope; surprised at the jogging of the paper against her body, our entertainer took it; and the hand disappeared from sight.

Whether this was part of the game or not I could not know. But as I in turn looked around the bright room with its postage-stamp black windows and drooping chandelier, I realized I had seen the hand before – or felt it, rather, on my journey up to find my niece Lou. It was smooth – and, as I had now seen, small, with a gap where the third and fourth fingers had been.

I believe the first moment of real fear I have suffered in my life was when I realized she was bringing it over to me now, my Maîtresse d'Hôtel, with the look of a conjuror about to pull a rabbit out of a hat, as I sat paralysed in the snowbound room, with its glittering crystal teardrops and night-blackened window panes. The first experience of true terror I have ever undergone was when I knew – somehow, but she backed up my hunch, oh yes she did! – that the letter was for me. I held my outstretched arm blindly upwards, as if to fend her off. But – 'Professor Sunderland, this is for you' – and her voice rang out like a circus whip. 'Do tell us what is inside!'

Here we were, the assorted guests at a harmless Christmas party, a party where a slightly unusual entertainment had been promised to take account of the bookish nature of some of those participating and to introduce to the works of the nineteenth and twentieth centuries' greatest author a selection of young girls more likely to be aficionados of 'chick lit' than connoisseurs of *The Golden Bowl*. Douglas McGill had promised a ghost story more chilling than *The Turn of the Screw*. And what had happened? The uncompleted short story had about as much potential for provoking terror as one of James's successors at Lamb House's literary efforts, E.F. Benson. McGill, who had obviously believed the exciting account from the Bell Street pedlar of Miss Bosanquet's visit to his father all those years ago – the manuscript in a chest and all the rest – was the sole member of our ill-assorted group who appeared satisfied by the words he had just read out. McGill, I was not displeased to see, appeared as bored as the others by the whole concept – ghosts, story – even Henry James himself, for he closed the Leon Edel volume he carried with him – a biography of the Master where brief mention of *The Beautiful Child* is made – and he closed it with an air of finality I had not seen demonstrated at any class or lecture. It had been his idea, though: he had made a fool of himself, the elderly satyr, and returning his hand to poor Mary's knee, as he now proceeded to do, he had the air of a dejected suitor. There may be nothing worse than failing to enthral an audience, as the Master knew so well. For those who 'can't keep it up' the outcome is bitter indeed.

Now I must decide. I had every reason to suppose that Digital Towers – or whatever this web-obsessed Edwardian pile is called – may be infinitely more haunted – yes, that is the term for the experience I suffered on the upper landing – than one could at first have thought possible. Do I tell my sister-in-law about the hand? Should I inform the young woman known as 'Jasmine' that I am surprised at her taking Mrs Archdean's name, when the recent reading was presumably the first time the relatively uncommon surname had been heard here?

Or should I simply leave, slip away from a house party turned sinister where I – so it seemed – had been singled out for whatever unpleasant prank the hosts wished to visit on me. I knew the humiliation of the television reality-show victim. Surely it was time to go.

❖ ❖

I took the letter into the hall and ran my thumbnail along the thick, cream-coloured paper until the envelope fell open and my name came up at me – this on thicker paper still, like (I couldn't help thinking) an insect embalmed in a chemical solution: long dead and almost unrecognizable.

But the letter was for me all right. I could hear the voices in the opulent drawing-room, of the audience just subjected to the Master's unfinished effort, *Hugh Merrow* or *The Beautiful Child*, and I thought I could pick out the mousy, rather aggressive woman who had introduced herself before the reading as Mrs Archdean. Sighing, discontented – was she going to try to tell us her own ending, had she contrived to learn from McGill about the agonies James had suffered in trying to complete what had seemed a rich and amusing tale – and had she taken a feminist route to understanding it, to explain his failure to empathize with the childless wife, for all his protestations to the contrary? Would one's students in future, with their fascination for their own 'space' and their Facebooks and the virtual identity of almost everything, insist on assuming the names of the characters invented by an author? How is one supposed to react? Must there be a charade, when all that is needed in understanding a work is a combination of intelligence and scepticism rarely found in the young these days? I knew I had offended the false Isabel Archdean. Perhaps I should go back in and sit with her amongst the glass-topped tables and the *objets de vertu*, all suspiciously like the junk you see displayed on a

Brighton stall at the Saturday Market. As an encouraging mentor I should press 'Jasmine' for her story. This could be incorporated into James's *Beautiful Child*. How much more post-postmodern could you get? I didn't of course. The letter was only a few lines long and written in an old-fashioned hand.

Dear Professor Sunderland,

I write to inform you that my great-aunt Mary Weld expressed a wish shortly before her death that any scholar interested in the facts surrounding the uncompleted tale *The Child* (or *The Beautiful Child*, or *Hugh Merrow*) should meet a descendant able to provide details of the strange happenings at Lamb House, Rye, in the summer of 1902.

I am the one to have been entrusted with the task. You will be admitted by the entrance to the Garden Room at ten minutes to midnight and should make your way to the powder room leading from the drawing-room, where I will await you. I give an undertaking that what I am about to divulge was known to nobody other than my aunt; and that it will devolve on you and no one else to spread – or bury – the truth about Henry James.

The letter was signed Philippa something-or-other; the Weld name had evidently been subsumed by the years, owing to marriages and succession of the male line. But I believed her.

And as I made my way from the pretentious

structure hired by my media partners and out into the snow I believed the niece of the Master's amanuensis, the colonial Miss Weld, even more wholeheartedly than before.

For a car, circa the first decade of the twentieth century – a Hispano Suiza, perhaps, or a Packard (I am no expert in these matters) – stood in the circular driveway. An old man sat at the wheel. He waved to me, and I climbed in. We set off for Rye.

~:· ·:~

It was not a long journey, but the whirling snow, the occasional gaps in the black sky where stars showed through as if burned there by smouldering blankets of dark cloud and the repetitive lines of trees – were they here in Henry James's time? I wondered, or were they planted after the Great War, a memorial to the platoons of soldiers who had lost their lives? – all provided a timeless quality at once restful and unnerving. I knew I was *en route* to Lamb House; but not as an ordinary visitor. It was as the passenger of the old man who drove me that I came; and he, surely, was a revenant from the days of *The Golden Bowl* and *The Wings of the Dove*. Mary Weld it was who had thrilled to the melodious tones of the Master as he dictated his impossible sentences, pausing only to lean against an escritoire, head in hands, when the correct word fled his mind and had to be coaxed back into existence; Mary Weld, or her niece, would supply the answer to our puzzle, and I would be left with the choice, as the present-day Miss Weld had put it, to broadcast or destroy the evidence surrounding the unfinished story.

A bitter cold had invaded the car, and I found myself shivering and then beginning to cough, always a dangerous sign for me in the winter. What was I doing here? Would it not have been better to allow the earnest reader from Paddington Basin to declaim Theodora's completion of the story and await the reactions of my celebrity book-panel partners. Miss Bosanquet, after all, had announced herself as a novice writer – and none are more ambitious than they when it comes to attention-grabbing prose, unreliable narrators and all. Very likely, with her long pre- and post-mortem acquaintanceship with the Master, she had half guessed already how Hugh Merrow fared with his clients; probably she had been amused, as I had, by the painter's declaration of hope that he could 'keep it up', when, with the benefit of hindsight, she had known perfectly well that he could not. No, Miss Bosanquet had been seriously let down – by McGill's impatient wave to the nervous bookseller, who had stepped from his stool in response, the budding author's manuscript tucked under his arm – and by my shake of the head, which indicated, as I had intended it to, that this parlour game had been a flop. If we had left her to expound on her ending – and if we had kept away from the acute psychological riddle posed by Henry James's inability to complete the story – I would surely not be in this ancient car now, shaken like a bag of bones as icy puddles were crossed and owls hooted uncannily overhead. I would not, dear reader, have been afraid.

For I was afraid as I had never been: I, Professor Jan Sunderland, creator of literary quizzes, editor of the definitive edition of M.R. James's ghost stories, was on my way to quiz the other James, discover his darkest secrets, open myself up to the tossing of volumes by poltergeists who lurked ahead of me, preparing for my arrival. Worst of all, I must subject myself to the pious ramblings of Miss Weld (or whatever her name was now). I must be on my guard, on this terrible night in a freezing house, not to betray the frivolous reason for my presence. I must demonstrate that I had come for the sake of literature, not to satisfy the vulgar appetites of television book shows. But I knew my chattering teeth and rheumy, weeping eyes would surely give me away as a desperate publicity seeker, a failed author in search of his character.

But my apprehensive thoughts were soon brought to a halt. For now I recognized the steep hill leading to the house where the Master had made himself – at first so happily – at home.

Let me continue with this account without placing your idea of what happened next before me. Permit me, I implore you, to show some originality in the spinning of this narrative (though there is nothing original left to say, and I prefer a revisionary version of an old tale to any effort by my students to 'make it new', I must confess). This time, however, I must beg for the sympathy and understanding of my audience – should I survive to tell the tale. And the reason, as any fraudster will know, is my insistence that what took place on that mist-coiled, bone-chilling night is actually what did happen. No auto fiction this; the story of Mary Weld gives us the true meaning of fear – of horror, yes – but more of a fear that transforms, paralyses, takes shadows for friends and a man as no more than twisted bedclothes. It was this fear that propelled me from the old car which had finally coughed itself silent; and it was horror, maybe, that had me shaking as I looked upwards and saw her there, in the window of Lamb House, old, with papery skin hanging like rows of dead pearls at her neck, her eyes closed in the cold white rays of a New Year moon.

This, surely, could not be the great-niece who had written to me – but the very question is meaningless; for there was no age she could have belonged in, the old lady I glimpsed above. All I know is that the iron gate swung open, and it was possible to walk alongside the Garden Room, where the Master loved to compose in summer, his secretary smiling, scooping up his falling words like so many buttercups in a meadow. A man, taller than myself, waved me to walk through into the frosted garden. His gloves were white and slightly too small for his hands is what I noticed as the car struggled bronchially, finally took the plunge and set off back down the hill towards ersatz Edwardiana and 1930s villas, with council houses and bungalows running in neat suffocating blocks beyond the fringes of the town. Was this normality? I no longer knew the period of history, the meaning of architecture which had so interested me once – for me, as the iron gate swung shut behind me, there was no dwelling other than this one anywhere. For I had entered the Master's world – every line of Lamb House spelled out his secrets and his own appalling fear.

I followed the tall man, whose face I had not yet seen. I knew only that I disliked him intensely – but I could not say why. His way of walking was slow, carefully thought out as if some unadmitted enemy lurked at corners; and when he at last turned to me at the top of the stairs, I had to hold my breath to prevent myself from calling out in disgust at the man's features. What was it in the bland expanse of closely shaved cheek or in the small, impudent eyes which seemed to dismiss me and any right I might have to enter the precincts, and how did I know (which I overwhelmingly did) that this man was the source of James's terror? But the knowledge held me in a vice; and we both stood immobile in our different positions until a quavering voice called from somewhere down the corridor 'Smith!' – so we both turned like automata and proceeded in the direction of the command. The manservant Smith, if this was he – didn't look round at me as he went, and I dreaded him doing so, for my entire body – or so I experienced it – shrank, each sense mortified, and forbade me to catch him up. If I found myself a shorter distance from his back I had to slow my own walk to stay a safe distance from the man. Then at the far end of a passage, leading off the first floor of the house, a door opened and a woman walked out. She was gracious, copper-haired. She came towards me with a smile.

The butler – as I assumed him to be – disappeared down a narrow corridor, and I was left alone with the woman who would dictate my future life.

∼∙∙ ∙∙∼

The woman in the closet (it was no more than seven feet square) stood facing me as I struggled to make sense of my surroundings and the strange personage I knew I must confront. I guessed, of course, that this tiny room had been the hiding place for the unfinished story – and I tried desperately to remember what the messenger from Paddington had read out from Theodora Bosanquet's account of coming in here. She had entered, I saw, from the drawing-room, not from a passage, as I had done; and the realization that Lamb House might in fact conceal many such rooms and even stories by the Master, abandoned out of shame, as he would put it, was dizzying indeed. Why had I been taken in here other than to inform my guide of the content of Miss Bosanquet's packet – the assumption being, of course, that 'Mr James' as his amanuenses invariably called him, had confided the reason for abandoning the tale to Miss Bosanquet, Miss Weld's successor? And how could I answer the inevitable question, when the fear that had gripped me on first approaching the house still paralysed my vocal chords and brought beads of sweat to my face and hands? How could I find a way out – back to the cosy banalities of my media friends – and away from the smell of death which, in my state of hysteria, I was sure I could identify?

Oh, it emanated from my inquisitor – there was no doubt about that. I could hardly look – and she stood only a few paces away, after all, so it was difficult *not* to look at this – this mutant, this woman who was crone, mature female and young lady fresh out of Cheltenham College all at the same time. Old – she was as old as the ancient figure who had gazed down at me when I walked along the lawn by the side of this apparently decorous and innocent building; and she was, like the Snow Queen, both a myth and the truth. As a young woman she would ensnare me and carry me through white fields and up into the sky. As the copper-haired woman who had greeted me silently as I walked along the passage behind the manservant Smith, she would inform me in a low resonant tone of her request for an answer to the impossible question. As a young girl, she would hang on my reply. And of course I had none – frivolously I had neglected to ask myself what the Master's sudden desire to complete *The Beautiful Child* actually signified at such a time since its conception and its commencement over half a century after his death? Was the subject matter, possibly, now considered permissible where once its selection would have caused offence? But, if so, why had he come through the Ouija board to demand of the elderly Miss

Bosanquet that she take his dictation one last time? If he didn't know what would befall him – or his reputation, at least, on the unearthing of the tale – why did he force poor Theodora to travel in bitter winter weather to the home where once he had lived unmolested by press or gossips, Lamb House in Rye? And, if he was in fact in some kind of heavenly sanctuary beyond the stars, how had he condoned the ghostly appearance of Mary Weld – for this, I had no doubt, was who and what stood before me. A phantom, a mirage – but, as I knew, an important presence in the little household in the Sussex town where Henry James invented his great, late fictions. By the time Miss Bosanquet took the post of secretary typist all the important works had been written. And Mary Weld had been responsible, in the case of *Wings of the Dove*, *The Golden Bowl* and the first pages of *The Beautiful Child*, for transcribing the words of the Master. It occurred to me for the first time that it was I who had come here to ask questions, not she; and as my brain cleared I saw that the fear I had suffered had obscured the ordinary fact of Miss Weld's great-niece – yes, copper hair and all, she was of our age – and that I must ask her urgently to explain HJ's reasons for abandoning the tale of a painter who could not, even if he had really wanted to, complete the task expected of him.

MARY WELD'S STORY

I came to Lamb House to work for Mr James in April 1901. I knew there had been a male typewriter named McAlpine, who had preceded me in London, and at first I was nervous that his skills had been much superior to mine – for I found a note in his handwriting in the Green Room desk here which boasted that 'the Screw had turned' one morning when his employer asked him to go faster; and he mentioned a total of words per hour which was infinitely greater than mine. Whether this alleged slowness of McAlpine had caused HJ to dismiss him I do not know; but he has always shown great respect in his dealings with me, and in the six years in which I had the privilege of transcribing his work – including corrections for the New York edition of his *œuvre*, along with two major novels – we seldom disagreed over anything. I had learnt not to suggest a word for Mr James, on the rare occasions he stopped in mid-flow and agonized over the correct one, and I believe my tactful silences were in fact a help to him as he composed – while I, in turn, gained a few moments of rest as the unspoken deliberations went on. Except on the occasion of a story for which, he informed me, he had been given the foundations by his friend the writer Paul Bourget; a story entitled first *The Child*, then *Hugh Merrow* and lastly *The Beautiful Child*. With this tale nothing seemed to go right; it felt, even as I typed, to be somehow uneasy, as if a certain kind of object was continually being forced into the wrong-sized receptacle – I cannot, unfortunately, put it more clearly than that. I showed no impatience while words were fought for and abandoned – and I was frequently asked to ring the bell for coffee – but even when he resumed and selected the phrase that was needed for the tale he would go back over my typed pages in the late afternoon and announce they must be thrown away or amended so radically that we had to start the next day right from the beginning. It was not my habit to make enquiries into the reasons for Mr James's decisions – and though I privately felt he had nothing to lose by jettisoning this piece of work (he was concurrently writing another story, *The Beast in the Jungle*, and had begun his great novel *The Wings of the Dove*) he seemed determined to make *The Beautiful Child* his priority. I thought this a wrong decision but of course said nothing to that effect.

By the summer of the year following (1902) it was possible to perceive that Mr James's health was declining rapidly. He complained of shortness of breath – and we no longer took walks together across the marsh (this quite a relief to me, I must confess, as a most unpleasant fellow writer, Ford Madox Hueffer, took pleasure in following us on our peregrinations. HJ and I went so far on one occasion as to hide in a ditch to escape his attentions! Perhaps selfishly I also welcomed the time off supplied by Mr James's lack of desire to walk; and thus – the summer was by turns violently rainy or unpleasantly sultry – I took to spending more time in Lamb House and its environs than I had been accustomed to do.

Before I continue I should explain that I had been from the very first surprised – even dismayed – by Mr James's choice of servants for his country residence. Little Russell Noakes, almost a dwarf but agile and helpful at all times and much jested about and liked by Mr James, caused no problems at all. As, indeed, was the case with Fanny . . . poor red-nosed Fanny, always sniffing about one injustice or another (she lived with her mother down the hill at Rye, if I remember correctly). Fanny would moan and talk as long as she was permitted to; and Mr James being deep in thought, I saved him as often as I could from her unwanted interpolations. I recall that I would from time to time smile at the probable reaction of Miss Petheridge in her secretarial agency in Victoria (it was she who had found me my place with Mr James) if she had been informed of the time I took over Fanny's chronic difficulties (she had twins, a boy and a girl, about four years old, always ailing and frequently brought to Lamb House owing to lack of care at home), a job for which I had most certainly not been hired.

❖ ❖

Nor did I consider it to be my place to report any misdeeds or questionable actions on the part of a staff member at Lamb House. Little Russell's day off was his own business and not that of his Master, even if he did return home like the unreliable Bobby Shafto, without so much as a bunch of blue ribbons after gambling his wages away at the fair. I kept myself to myself and felt grateful – increasingly so by the summer of 1902, I must say – for the comfortable little cottage where Mr James had found me a reasonably well-appointed pair of rooms and a friendly uninterfering landlady, a sister of Dr Skinner. There was a tacit understanding between us that Mr James's health or daily habits would not be discussed, and a plate of scones and a workmanlike pot of tea was usually shared between us in an amicable silence.

That summer, though, I found myself tested to my furthest limits by Mr and Mrs Smith, the cook and butler at Lamb House. It was just over a year that I had been there, and, to be frank, I had found myself surprised at their lack of charm. This is more polite than they deserved: Mrs Smith had a permanently heightened colour and wore dresses so – presumably – carelessly donned that a button or belt could always be seen to be missing, she was rotund, not to say mountainous, and the effect was altogether unsavoury. And Mr Smith, well, Professor, you have already seen Mr Smith I believe. He showed you in and enabled you to find me here.

Please do not interrupt, Professor. You must know

that those who serve Henry James, in either fiction or fact, are immune to the vagaries of life: the mistakes and accidents, the mortal illnesses that come to carry us off to another world. For Mr James, however, every friend was a friend for life – and for longer if they figured in his novels.

Mr Smith was even less appealing than his wife. As you have noted, he had a peculiarly unpleasant gaze, both cunning and malevolent, s and it was hard for me to understand why they were so treasured. They had been sixteen years in Mr James's service – not all at Lamb House, certainly not: the first complaints I heard shortly after my arrival came from Mrs Smith, who informed me that De Vere Gardens, where they had looked after Mr James, had all the advantages (near shops, being in London, etc. etc.), while Lamb House, packed with guests as it frequently was in summer, demanded too much work, and the emptiness of the house in winter brought depression and a desire to escape the marsh.

I cannot explain why I failed to notice the obvious affliction of the Smiths; all I can say is that I found them both so repulsively unpleasant that I would not allow myself any speculation about their state of mind. Why should I become involved in the couple's lives when my connection with the place was entirely due to Mr James? I it was who acted as amanuensis to the great man; it was my happy fate to accompany him as he composed, like a pianist with a world-renowned singer. This is how I saw our relationship: he dictated and I followed, sometimes as he was apt to point out himself, with an uncanny sense of what he was about to say, before he said it. There are other parallels with a musical experience – for to toil at a desk and find Mr James's melodious voice float over one was akin to finding oneself a small but vital part of an orchestra.

The first time I seriously wondered if I should speak to Mr James on the subject of the Smiths, I concluded that I should not; and to this day I rue the decision. If I had come out with my suspicions – even, as they became, my accusations – I might have obviated the need for urgent medical attention demonstrated by my employer on the day of the fatal luncheon party. The whole awful business could have been swept away – or under the carpet at least, until Mr James's special friend Mr Anderson left Lamb House, and the writer T. Bailey Saunders, a man of many words (and a great moustache to conceal or promote them), had departed on his bicycle for a trip down the coast. But I said nothing; and Mr James, I am sorry to say, became exposed to the curiosity of the county, only just succeeding in his attempt to refuse the local constabulary the opportunity to publicize the squalid event even further.

The two accounts are therefore not connected, though they became so with the chaos of the Smiths' departure, and I feel to this day that Mr James believes me partly culpable for their dismissal. Not fair, I know; but one must remember that he had seemed ever since my first days at Lamb House to like the unpre-possessing pair quite inordinately. 'I owe a great deal to

Mr and Mrs Smith,' Mr James would say, and he would smile reminiscently, as if (highly improbably as I believe they were illiterate) it was they who created some part of his fictions or had transcribed them (also highly improbable).

The staff at Lamb House – Fanny, Russell Noakes and Ned the gardener – were paid on Fridays, in guineas, and these I distributed at the end of the day. They went in a black Gladstone bag where I stored Mr James's sentences – those that were imponderable, at least, and in need of his scrutiny in an evening's reading and checking.

On Friday 11th July I discovered that the small gold coins had vanished from my bag – there were three in all, and a half-sovereign, unnoticed by the thief, still languished in a fold of the lining.

It was a hot, airless day; and, seizing the bag, I went over to the french windows of the Garden Room. It was not what I should have done, I know: the theft needed to be reported to the authorities – and not least to Mr James. The unconsidered move then spelt out further ill fortune for me, as Mr Smith and his wife now approached the window from outside and waved at me with their usual expressions of friendship, an assumption that was totally unacceptable to me. The key (Mr Smith, as butler, had keys to every room and cellar in Lamb House, a fact which made me even more grateful to be lodged away with Dr Skinner's sister in town and not in a house where Smith could roam, if he so pleased, into every room) jiggled in the lock of the Garden Room french windows a few seconds longer, then turned and the Smiths stood facing me. This was a situation I found most undesirable – for I was certain it was they who had taken the money from my bag. If questioned, they would lay the blame elsewhere – and this they proceeded to do, but only after throwing me into confusion by implying that it was I who was somehow to blame for an action of which they had not been accused and – unless obviously guilty – could not be charged for.

'So when is your departure, miss?' said Mrs Smith.

'Yes, when are you going?' her husband now enquired. 'We'll have Ned ready to take you to the station for the London train. At least, that is what the Master informed us . . . And here the rascal fell silent. He had come perceptibly closer to me – without apparently moving – and I was reminded of the childhood games I used to play with my brothers and sisters. Tom Tiddler's Ground or Grandmother's Footsteps.

I backed away – but I had reason much later to feel gratitude that this disgustingly cunning and scheming man had had the impertinence to come up so close. For I smelt his breath – it floated over me and around me – it was unspeakably vile, like the stink of the corpse of a decomposing animal, so I thought, and yet it came not from hedgerow, field or marsh – but from this man himself, from deep inside him, where he rotted physically and morally. The worst part was that he brought his wife – who now walked up to me with a mock-contrite air: she often, I noticed, assumed the guise of a maltreated woman, albeit with a carefully assumed abashed look on her face – to make his pleas and arrange his horrible satisfactions. It was impossible to stand there a minute longer – but, as if I defended my position at Lamb House in the face of the Smiths' certainty of my imminent departure, I continued to stand. It was I who could have been in the dock: without a word being said I stood accused of a theft and was now the unhappy possessor of the knowledge that the true criminals had reported my 'crime' to our employer. The terrible couple had triumphed over me, and I no longer even knew what to say.

'Miss Weld?' The impasse was eased by the arrival of Mr James at the Garden Room window. 'I shall change my schedule for today,' he announced, and I feared his shortness of breath had worsened as a result of a recent excitement. 'We shall have the story . . .' and here he glanced with evident happiness in the direction of his two foul servants. 'No, let me put it this way. I consider the story of Hugh Merrow to be an important addition –'

'*The Beast in The Jungle*,' I found the courage to put in. 'You have only a few pages more, Mr James, to complete it . . .'

My tone was unconvincing: perhaps my relief at finding I had not been dismissed by my employer (and, after all, he had confided in Mr and Mrs Smith for sixteen years and I had only been twelve or thirteen months at Lamb House) had given me an air of artificiality. But the Smiths had clearly not been believed, at least – and they must have known they had registered a false piece of information. I might tell Mr James, the man they referred to as Master; but I decided against this course of action – concord reigned in my hours of dictation, and I was sure I was not expected to leave the premises as they had forecast.

But I was not to rest quiet after my reinstatement (in my mind at least) as a valued member of the Lamb House entourage. For Mr James, who had never, in my knowledge at least, expressed an interest in poor Fanny the housemaid – it was I who performed various charitable actions to aid the wretched young woman – now proceeded to speak of her in the same breath as a recently embarked on and set aside short story.

'I speak of *The Child* – you have the pages, Miss Weld!' continued HJ. 'I have informed Fanny the housemaid that I shall need them before I recommence.'

'*The Child*?' I said, aware I sounded foolish – even, perhaps, giving fresh ammunition to the Smiths in their efforts to rob me and send me away from Rye.

'*Hugh Merrow* then' – and a hand was held out to me as if in supplication. '*The Beautiful Child,* you have filed it somewhere, doubtless, Miss Weld. But first I must show you the beacon of my inspiration' – and with a nod Mr James indicated to the Smiths that they should leave the room. 'Come out here with me. It is hardly raining at all.' And, still breathless, Henry James led me into the garden, green and damp as it was. We walked under poplars to the far wall, HJ panting, I am sorry to say, with his effort of walking even that short distance. Then, by a row of espaliered fruit trees against the wall, we saw them. Golden-haired, blue-eyed, playing happily by the side of a flower-bed with a pair of small shovels – 'Mrs Archdean will be pleased indeed when her fondest wish comes true,' Mr James remarked. 'A child deserving the brush of Hugh Merrow – and, if I may say so, the pen of Henry James.'

'But' – in my attempt to conceal my anxiety I fairly shouted at my employer – 'which of them will you choose, sir? The boy or the girl?' And there, Professor, is where he left me, for T. Bailey Saunders could be seen at the gates into the garden and there was little the Master disliked more than a lack of hospitality.

PROFESSOR JAN
SUNDERLAND

Now I saw Mary Weld in the extremities of old age. Her arm, as it reached to me for a farewell, was so transparently veiled in skin that the blue veins, like dark grapes, were clustered near the visible bone – and her face, propped like a marionette's on her other arm, appeared one-dimensional, a sheet of paper where too much had already been written and all was finally about to be erased.

She was tired; she would continue the next day with the extraordinary story of Lamb House; she bade me good-night and hoped I would sleep well. The door in the panelling of the tiny room swung aside to let her pass. And I – my policy of total exposure being essential for the further recounting of this exploration of the aspirations and terrors of Henry James – stood for a moment rooted to the ground, the icy fear which had gripped me at first sighting of the manservant Mr Smith returning to keep me there several minutes.

I remembered Miss Bosanquet and her account of entering the powder closet from the drawing-room, and after twiddling about with catches and snibs concealed in the skirting-board I found myself free – in a cold, unlit room that smelt of damp and mice, admittedly, but free.

The body, even in a state of paralysis, demands food, and I hurried down the main staircase (I had no wish to bump on the service stairs into either of the Smiths) and made my way to the back of the house. To find the kitchen was encouragingly easy. There was even a smell of something like vegetable broth – what my high-stepping young ladies at Media Mansions would doubtless call minestrone – and this was exactly what I needed: a good hearty soup on the bleakest and most dreary night of the year. I went through a green baize door, saw the kitchen with its old-fashioned great pans lying before me, several chairs pulled out from the table and a figure at the above ladling and stirring. This was a woman in the long black skirt and white apron of female servants at the turn of the twentieth century; her hair was up in a bun and could be seen even at a distance to be shockingly greasy and unkempt; she muttered as she poured the soup into tin plates. Russell Noakes, willing and good-humoured as Miss Bosanquet had described him, smiled at me as I came in a few steps and paused as a shaft of rank-smelling steam obscured my entrance. Then the little fellow danced up to me, all of his five feet expressing eagerness to make me at home. Yet once again I found myself unable to move either backwards or forwards. A terrible sense overtook me that suspicions which had lain dormant for the span of our frivolous 'Henry James Parlour Games' at Media Mogul Villas were now about to be confirmed. My head felt it was going to burst. And I prayed, while dodging young Russell's proffered plate of stew gone rotten over incalculable lengths of time in a filthy kitchen, that I would be proved wrong – and would then be able to leave the famous writer's house in Rye and, if necessary, walk back to the sham palace we had all taken in the expectation of passing a jolly New Year.

But it was not to be. The woman at the stove turned but did not see me, and in her surprise at feeling a presence – and dismay at sensing a ghostly visitor – she dropped the ladle into the malodorous mixture on the range. She gave a groan; perhaps she had half expected to find a denizen of our times here who would rescue her, or so her sound of despair told me – some magical solution was prayed for but did not materialize. For standing before was a woman transformed, hideous but recognizable – my Salome of the January sales, she who had shown the greatest scepticism of all our theories, the high-booted, impossibly short-skirted friend in Prada.

'Fanny, you can go home now,' the minuscule Russell informed the woman I had – yes I admit it – fancied in a previous incarnation at Digital Towers.

'You're expected here at 8 a.m. to do the breakfast,' Russell went on as Fanny/Salome and I stood, she still unaware of me, by the black dirt-encrusted stove.

It was clear that these words were all the maid expected. 'And the Master says you're to bring the children' were the houseboy's last words, as she walked to the kitchen door, briefly passing me. Again, I suffered the intolerable sensation of being there but not seen. Then she was gone.

✧ ✧

I cannot give a clear account of the rest of that terrible night. Here I was, in the house made real to me long before I came here by the words of James's biographer Leon Edel – and by Miss Bosanquet's charming booklet, published by the Hogarth Press in 1924, a straight-forward admission to the House of Genius, with its considerate Master, eight secretarial tables and all. Long before my first visit – the local estate agent in Sandwich had advertised the house for rent by a suitable couple (ha! what would they make of the present incumbents, now I had begun to see the powers which had taken over here) – a couple who would know the works of the previous occupant of Lamb House, be aware of the guests who had thronged the great man's drawing-room and show the garden, a particular favourite of James, who liked to look out of his window and see an English gardener at work. I had visited, as a prospective tenant, and my credentials had been good. I was a Professor of English at —— University, after all and had produced, in the distinguished American periodical *Raritan*, an essay on James's Anglophilia, but I'd had no intention of leaving my home town. In reality I simply wanted to view the house and be taken seriously while I was doing so.

I will not dwell on the unpleasant effect on one's nerves it can have to revisit a delightful location and find it fallen into – if this is not too fanciful an expression – evil hands. Lamb House, on that night when it became clear to me that the spirits which haunted it had taken control of the place entirely, restricting and dictating all movement, curtailing a freedom without which we can none of us breathe or function – Lamb House, on that night of the New Year Full Moon, was as sly, malignant and corrupt as its vile spirit inhabitants. No prayer or mantra could save the incoming traveller: to abandon hope was the only option available – and on doing so, I had little doubt, one would fall for ever into the grip of the cook and butler, the Quint and Jessel (as I now saw) who had terrorized the children in James's masterpiece *The Turn of the Screw*. They had continued, after becoming a part of their master's removal to the country, to exercise their dreadful talents in the house at Rye; and our little party in the Edwardian house down the road – devoted as it was to the study and (faintly ridiculous) worship of James simplified for a television arts programme – was a prime target for them. We were a danger to the ghostly couple, as they prowled the house and its environs for new victims. Children, innocent and unaware, would never grow up here – there must be dozens of Mileses and Floras who had not gone beyond seven or ten years of age.

The moon was casting a bluish light into the empty bedrooms as I stumbled down the first-floor passage and, thinking myself courageous indeed, flung open their doors. I was conscious, in a way I had never known before, of a vast exhaustion as it crept over me, bringing with it a deep cold that penetrated as far as the bone. Why the place was unfurnished, I could not even speculate – for it was impossible to know, as with so many 'historic' homes in England, which era we were in. Even to think of poor Salome transformed to a drudge was unbearable to me then.

At last I reached the final bedroom in the passage – it opened out on to the principal landing of the house and would boast a fine view of the garden and the hills beyond had not the snow turned to sleet, eddying like a giant white brush, obscuring all details of either; and I turned the handle and looked in. There must be some exhibition, I thought, to do with Henry James and his artefacts, for this room at least had been prepared carefully – or artfully, perhaps, in expectation of a paying visitor. A four-poster bed was made up, with linen sheets and large plumped pillows; a mahogany cupboard stood open, displaying a selection of tweed jackets, knickerbockers and the like; and a small table by the side of the bed was laid out, perhaps in readiness for a writer's thoughts before breakfast, with pen, a blotter and a leather paper-holder with discreetly engraved address inscribed on each letter.

My exhaustion turned to gratitude. Someone somewhere knew I needed comfort – and, beyond that, compliments on my intimate knowledge of the work of the Master were clearly in evidence. A glass of fresh orange juice on the small painted commode on the far side of the bed showed consideration for my recent hideous experiences. Breakfast would be brought as soon as it was light, I had no doubt; and the small library on shelves either side of a fireplace in which a controlled blaze gave out much-needed warmth demonstrated that my invisible host knew all that had been written about him and his great fictions since the time of his death.

I wanted desperately to sleep; but first, going to the bookcases, I pulled out a volume, circa 1970 I would say – and the words I had sought almost jumped out at me, causing me to back towards the four-poster and surrender myself to its goose-feather-filled expanse. They were the words of my hero, Leon Edel, the biographer who knew more about James than any other. Something told me, as I fell back into the soft, embroidered pillows, that by scanning these words I would understand what had caused my fear.

The fire crackled; a bell rang somewhere, perhaps summoning one of James's guests to breakfast – Lily Norton, maybe, or Hendrik Andersen, the handsome young sculptor proffered by daring literary types as the actual lover of the Master, when Edel would most certainly deny the possibility, insisting always on James's total chastity. Then there was silence, comfortable country-house silence . . . I lay even further back between the curtains hanging from the four-poster, and finding the book an unpleasant weight – my frozen bones and state of exhaustion were doubtless the cause of an unprecedented rejection of a work on the subject of Henry James – I succumbed to the necessity of sleep.

But what a sleep it proved to be! I knew I was not awake – but I was fully aware, also, that some foreign force had taken over my mind, my vitals, my heart. I was powerless, as my new occupants feasted on my porous, vulnerable identity to banish them or find the strength to eject them forcefully from what I had always recognized as my self.

It started with the sounds of someone breaking into the room. I opened my eyes – but I remained unconscious and, worst of all, cognizant that I could make no move against my enemy. He – maybe two of them, for I heard barked orders on the far side of the door – was pressing his shoulder against the mahogany portal which only a short time earlier had appeared the most welcoming, reassuring sight to greet my eyes since the whole Lamb House nightmare began. As I lay in the high-masted ship that was the Master's bed I heard the undeniable sound of someone – maybe the same someone – bearing down on the lock and bolt from the passage outside.

What came next was, as I see now, the turning point in the dreadful assault: the lock (or perhaps another part of the ingenious door furniture which had protected the room's inhabitant from the outrage of burglary or personal attack) gave with a sickening crunch – and the massive door swung open.

Is it possible to become drunk without drinking? Are there occasions when a disturbed mind leaves its impression in a receptive brain, even a century after its sufferings at the hands of a missionary of the Devil? I cannot know; but, as the terrible figure approached me I knew myself to be fighting hallucinations and strange dreams, and I smelt the alcohol as it swirled around me. I tried to rise from the bed, but I was giddy and fell back on the bolsters. Two fireplaces, two of everything my eye fell on, brought greater confusion – even my own hand, pale and lifeless on the counterpane, rose up to me in double digits. I had been poisoned, and the whisky smell grew unbearably strong, so that I gagged and then cried out like a child, as the aura intensified and the awful figure came up closer to where I lay.

For who was this man, and why did he seem so familiar? I could not face the recognition I now experienced – and pushed away – and was yet one more time anaesthetized by the strong spirits that were distilled all around me. I knew that the opening of the door would all too abjectly signify the end: in the grey, grizzled figure who now gloated down at me I would find the agent of Henry James's shame.

I saw myself: grey, grizzled, with hands covering my face. The hands dropped, and I saw the face was mine but not mine; on the left hand two fingers were missing.

⁙ ⁙

I must have fainted – and when I regained consciousness I saw the drawn, papery features of Mary Weld. We were in the little powder room; she had placed a blanket under me, and I dimly perceived that a fire of sorts had been laid in the minuscule grate; a bunch of twigs fizzled damply, extruding a strong smell of neglected woodland, and a solitary pine cone lay against the bars. Otherwise the strange, repellent atmosphere of Lamb House was as it had been before I walked along the corridor and found myself in the Master's bedroom. And whether it was my imagination or not I could not tell – this time the faint aroma of stale alcohol lingered even here, growing stronger with the rising of the wind and the accompanying rush of hail and snow down the narrow – and obviously unswept – chimney. I coughed: the fire that failed to prosper could at least ignite my lungs; and it was only when a beaker of water was handed down to me that I was able to prop myself on one arm. Oh, I did not examine my hands: my memory of the oneiric horror of my visit to the chamber of the author of *The Turn of the Screw* was still close for me, and I dreaded the return of his fear – for this it was, I was sure: it was connected to the evil story and the evil servants who had administered to him at the time of writing his terrifying novella – and I looked up at the desk where Miss Weld now sat, custodian of Henry James's nightmares, keeper of the flame where I and so many others had worshipped over the years. Last night she had been tired, exhausted by her great age and her dreadful secrets; today, I realized, she was the young and fresh-faced amanuensis I had seen in early photographs of James at weekend house parties or strolling alone by the side of pleached trees, with Mary Weld always a few paces behind. The ancient lady had gone – or had been expected and therefore dreamt up my me – and as her descendant began to speak, I felt the first rays of a January sun as it succeeded the hail and snow and came slanting in through the window in the drawing-room, the concealed door having been left ajar. I prepared myself to listen; and I fought down the return of the sensation which rose in me time and again in waves of a freezing terror that would never release me until I knew the truth behind the Master's inability to complete the tale.

'We tried three times to bring *The Beautiful Child* to life,' began Mary Weld; and as she spoke I pulled myself in to a sitting position, from head to feet occupying the entire floorspace of the tiny cabinet. 'But however hard we tried, the games the servants had played with the children had finally removed their breath – their spark – even their last consciousness had been irrevocably altered by the instructions they, puppet-like, obeyed.'

'The children? Both of them?' I said, my own voice so low I could hear the mounting gusts of wind as they came to batter the long windows of the drawing-room. 'Was it not one perfect child the author wanted, to satisfy the painter and his clients?' And I thought, as Miss Weld looked at me across the desk with an unbearable compassion, that all the research and meticulous attention to the text in the world never can bring back the past with accuracy. There is always someone – in this case, another child – who has not been mentioned or becomes a lost footnote in a dead biographer's tome.

'Fanny – you saw her in the kitchen earlier.' And as I shuddered at the memory of my smart, modern student transformed to a slattern – 'Fanny brought her children with her on certain days, Professor, when there was no one to care for them, a sadly frequent occurrence. As I informed you – and you should remember this, for it is of great significance – they were twins – a boy and a girl. Of outstanding beauty, and four years old as I remember well, for their birthday fell on the 2nd of July 1901, the day the Smiths were released from employment at Lamb House by their master' – and now it was her turn to shudder – 'the day Mr and Mrs Smith, spectral in their appearance, as Mr James wrote in a letter to Mrs William which was first dictated to me: he was too distracted, you understand, to hold a pen – the day they left here for good. Not before –' she added in a grim tone which transformed itself to currents of icy fear down my back and legs – 'not before they had caused the deaths of the children they first humiliated and abused.'

'And – and how did they . . .' I heard my voice falter. I coughed, and the fire, properly alight at last, devoured the pine cone like a black fruit.

'They caused one child to kill another,' Mary Weld said. Her tone was moderate, she might have been explaining the rules of a harmless game, such as four-year-old children play when they find themselves in a strange house alone. There was no heart in the woman, despite her hatred for the manservant and his wife, I realized: she felt for only one person in the world, and that was her employer, the man with the 'melodious voice', Mr James.

'But . . .' I struggled with the knowledge that Miss Bosanquet also had been in love with the Master. Would both typists defend Henry James's actions – or lack of them – to the end? 'But . . .' I said, and continued in as reasonable a manner as could be expected, that I would very much like to know how the double deaths had come about – and how the owner of this distinguished building, the great Henry James, had permitted the children to go unsupervised for what must have been a good length of time without trying to save them from the consequences of their ghastly game? The unwelcome thought, that composition – novel-writing if you like – is prone to remove humane considerations from the practitioner was impossible to ignore.

'Mr James was waiting for his friend Mr Bailey Saunders to arrive for luncheon on the 2nd of July that year, when the . . . the accident took place,' Mary Weld replied. 'He was apprehensive that Mr Saunders, who was a man of very slender talent, would exhaust him and fail to leave at a civilized hour. Mr James's true friend Mr Anderson was due to arrive from Italy the next day. He wished, naturally, to keep as fresh as possible.'

'So had you been . . . taking dictation that morning,

Miss Weld?' I asked while feeling myself to have entered the works of Arthur Conan Doyle rather than the imaginative sphere of Henry James. 'He was tired already. Perhaps . . . he failed to hear the cries of the children . . . ?'

'The half-written story *The Beautiful Child* had been abandoned once and for all that morning,' the secretary replied plainly. 'He had thought, when Mr and Mrs Smith first showed him Fanny's two cherubs' – and here, I saw, the already prim lips of Miss Weld curled further into an expression of disapproval and disgust – 'he had imagined that the gender of the winning candidate to be a sitter to the much-praised Hugh Merrow would be decided without any further doubt. He would not choose between the boy and the girl: he would use first one and then the other as models for the portrait. But as it was, he was left a problem as insoluble as the one he had suffered previously. "What shall I do, Miss Weld?" he cried to me when little Russell Noakes had run out of the house, eyes staring like a buck rabbit, to break the news of the children's game and its terrible end. Mr James was distraught. But neither I nor he could come up with the answer, though earlier in the day, when the Smiths brought the little angels into his study, it did seem that a solution had been arrived at. Finally, of course, this turned out not to be the case . . .'

'Mr James did nothing,' I said.

'He left the children to fight it out, as it were . . . for

they must have believed there was still some competition between them. And there was,' Mary Weld said simply. 'No real solution had been arrived at after all . . .'

There was an uncomfortable silence while I pondered the replies to my questions. Surely if a doctor or surgeon had been rushed to the house it might have been possible to save the lives of the two innocents? It seemed foredoomed, this dreadful occurrence; and the lack of composure in my silence (as for Miss Weld, she seemed perfectly as calm as before) must have showed only too clearly, for the worthy amanuensis now leant towards me with a confidential air. 'You must have been aware in your studies of the great author, Professor, that the girls in his unsurpassable stories are likely to endure, despite the vicissitudes visited on them by the plot and manner of execution. Boys, on the other hand, are more frail: they are liable to heart attacks and nervous collapses and seldom survive the tale devised for them.'

I have to admit that I was flabbergasted by this. People – flesh and blood, children, no less, were seen to be less important than characters in books! Their lives, if not suitable for the telling of a tale, worthless! 'Miss Weld . . .' I put in here, for a further silence had descended, and I knew myself damned if I did not voice my deadly serious objections. 'Mary!' I continued, and returned to my own century as I spoke. 'I came here with the expectation of discovering the truth behind an unfinished story by Henry James. I must demand that you . . .' – and here my voice did indeed falter again, and

I felt the superiority of the woman on the far side of the desk from me – 'I must insist on knowing exactly how they did die.'

Now the miniature fire, as if bursting with indignation, gave one last flare up into the sooty black of the chimney-piece before subsiding dead into the grate. The sound disturbed us both for a second or two, and then Mary Weld spoke. 'You have heard, Professor, of Russian roulette,' came quietly now in a shaking voice. 'Only one true cartridge is placed in the chamber of the gun. The rest are blanks.'

'Yes, of course,' I said; but I felt the fear come to seize my legs and then creep upwards to my throat, as I tried to speak. 'How . . . how could two four-year-old children play such a game? How . . .'

'Mr and Mrs Smith taught them. The girl fired first, and the boy was shot in the hand.'

'The hand?' I said.

'Yes. He lost the two middle fingers of his left hand,' Miss Weld said in a matter-of-fact tone. 'Then he aimed the gun at his sister.' At last there seemed to be a muffled sob, somewhere deep in Mary Weld. 'She fell and then died by the banister, the last step from the ground. But she knew it was her turn and now with her last strength she pulled the trigger. She had a deadly aim, as very young children sometimes show. The bullet killed her brother instantly.'

❖ ❖

To retrace one's steps in the wake of shock – a crisis, if you like, in the very fundaments of one's being – can be compared to the effect the rereading of a great classic can have on both the brain and the body's resilience. I recognized, as I pulled myself from my chair in the infernal cupboard where *The Beautiful Child* had languished for over a century – where first Miss Weld and then Miss Bosanquet had ensured the unfinished tale remained as hidden as the secret means of access to the closet and where I had encountered for the first time the lineaments of fear – the after-shudder that had come with the first devouring of the great Jorge Luis Borges or James Joyce. I had wanted more; yet I wished desperately to run from the seismic effect the new masters had brought with them – and I had considered myself to be safe with Henry James. I would not stand lost in any wasteland; I would not weep and howl; with the urbane, ever-considerate lord of Lamb House, I would be protected from the modern, while avoiding the charge – if, say, I had been teaching the works of Alfred Lord Tennyson – of marooning myself in the past.

I walked; I left the woman, now stooped and grey, at her desk in the powder room off the drawing-room; and one last glance over my shoulder showed her untouched by my departure and lifeless and ancient, a figure in a costume museum, made of no more than stuffing and rags. I felt the power return to my body as I went across the room with its panelled walls and windowpanes now bright and sparkling in an interlude of the sun. I half ran, to catch the minutes before snow and sleet descended once more. For I knew now that I must return to my guests and rescue those who were in need – or even in danger. The main staircase, for all its awful hauntings, existed only to carry me at speed down into the hall. And here – as grateful as I have ever been in my life for anything – I stopped by the door to the telephone room and then went in.

Before I recount the details of my return to the hired monstrosity where I feared my poor niece Lou must lie close to death in her four-poster and my sister-in-law Mary, her face now, in my new under-standing, a mask of concupiscence as the odious McGill kept her close by him, I should explain briefly that the story of Mr and Mrs Smith on that day in early July has been spelt out by biographers and historians and needs little further from me. I must stress that servants of the dead greats receive little attention from those who write about the immortals: not included in the index, they are often overlooked altogether. The Smiths were a slight exception: it is true that they have no existence at the back of recent books about Henry James – but Leon Edel gives some space to the fact that the manservant and his wife were at Lamb House – and had been sixteen years with their master (who, as if to give a cautious reference in the event of their leaving his employ) described them in a letter to his sister-in-law as 'a queer mixture of alcohol and perfection'. Mrs Smith's sister, called to come to Rye and pack up the belongings of her drunken sibling, was housekeeper to the poet laureate Alfred Austin. There was respectability, as well as excess, in the family, then – but more than that is not recorded, and the couple vanished into obscurity after their banishment on the 2nd of July.

I lifted the telephone receiver and found myself giving the number (Rye 1) to an operator whose accent and courtesy informed me that I could not escape the first years of the twentieth century so easily. I was connected after what seemed an age – and this filled with the voices and sounds so movingly described by Marcel Proust in his *Temps Perdu* lyrical descriptions of the young women at the telephone switchboard. I confess that hearing my former foe, the brash young woman I had nicknamed Salome, brought tears of relief to my eyes. For I had seen what a writer's powerful imagination could do, and I had feared the girl would be stranded in the basement kitchen of Lamb House in eternity, that she would continue for ever as a maid called Fanny whose two children had suffered torture and finally death at the hands of the butler and the housekeeper, Mr and Mrs Smith.

'How're you doin'?' came in Salome's maddening American mockney. 'When're you comin' back, Jan?'

I stepped back into the hall like a man newly in love. The sun had been replaced by scurrying clouds, but I had no fear of walking back drenched to the skin if necessary. I understood that those I had left in the mock Detmar Blow confection a few miles down the road from the Master's home in Rye might be transformed in one way or another – and I was ready for it. Those who were no more than innocent participants in a New Year's Eve quiz game would have left by train for London, I reckoned; those guilty of the crimes of cupidity, exploitation and betrayal manifested by the great author's protagonists might at first be unrecognizable. But, as I say, I was well prepared for my battle – and if it was to be waged against the man of genius I had taught and revered all my adult life, so be it. People, as I now knew, were more important than characters in books.

The storm caught me as I panted up the last stretch of cobbled hill to the virtual reality of my hosts' Big Brother nightmare. Hailstones the size of the proverbial golf ball took their aim at my head (I am, unfortunately, bald). A mean deluge of icy rain came down to soften the after-effects of being shot at by an amateur sniper – for this was how my mind registered the attack. But the more liquid form of ice caused the greater discomfort, trickling and then pouring down my neck after penetrating the collar of my coat. That I myself might be unrecognizable to the guests I had left behind did occur to me – but Salome, dear Salome of the discount and the vintage revival, had known my voice, and I prayed she would be there to greet me on arrival.

I must have been about fifty yards from the house when I saw, through the spectacular shower of rock-hard ice balls which still descended on me and around me, that a woman was in the front garden (this replete with the dreary shrubs deemed essential to those horrific institutions the care home and the prep school) and that she held a bundle in her arms.

Exhausted as I was, I increased my pace – and as I came nearer I saw the car and its ancient driver. It was the car that had ferried me to the infernal torture chamber of the Master's house. And the woman – yes, she was Mrs Archdean, formerly Jasmine – pulled open a door at the back of the vehicle and climbed in. She saw me as I skirted an obstreperous rhododendron, and she leant forward and tapped the driver's shoulder. Then the ghostly chariot coughed into life and lurched down the steep street leading away from us and towards the centre of Rye – and Lamb House.

'So they will all go there,' I said aloud, and my lips froze as I spoke. And they will never return, I thought. They will be his for ever. And I wept hot tears and knew that, like the rain which came down still, they would turn hard and freeze. I, like the rest, would never get back to real life. And as I saw the black glass of the windows in the media money-spinners' palace I knew they had already gone: young Lou, whose baby had been taken in order to finish the story; her mother Mary or Madame Merle; the dreadful McGill who was the spoiled, petulant Gilbert Osmond, a fop who feigned love for young Isabel Archer and married her for her money . . .

The house was as empty as I had known it would be. The stool where the middle-aged bibliophile from

Paddington had stood to read aloud from Miss Bosanquet's diary had been kicked over. Remains of the fancy array of canapés the media gang prefer to wholesome food lay abandoned on the dining table. Flung on to an armchair were the maid Fanny's clothes – it was as if a sudden eviction order had emptied the media centre, which, like its occupants, had turned out to be a figment of a third-rate imagination.

I stood in the hall and gazed up at the staircase which had led me to Lou's room. Thunder had come to join the evil orchestra of gale and gust, and an ecliptic darkness fell, leaving the unlit house as black as its imitation Gilbert Scott windows. I turned to find my way back to the front door, but I was afraid I would stumble. I waited and was glad the lightning which now came right in to the vaulted hall had not been waiting also – for me, for its final, fatal strike.

The figure at the top of the stairs could only just be made out in the dark. It was coming down – that I knew – it had a face, I knew, a face that was the Master's and also mine, and yet it belonged to neither of us.

It reached the bottom step. The house was silent now, the thunder had gone and the rain and hail had ceased.

It came across the hall to me. I took the hand in mine and ran my finger across the soft, yielding gap where once its third and fourth digits had been. The figure covered his face now with his other hand, and we stood there together in the hall.

The fire came in a red glow. I thought at first it must be emanating from electrical equipment: the 'Camera! Action!' I had grown used to in my television lectures on Henry James and his world would come next and ghosts would disperse – I would believe I was waking from a dream.

But the crackling and snapping, the whoosh of the flames as they spread through the deadly shrubs outside, soon convinced me that the blaze must have started in the attic, where faulty wiring in Edwardian times produced only too often a burnt-out shell for the proud owner. There was nothing artificial about the light the fire cast – and no special effects in the sudden ominous crunch when the hall itself succumbed to the thrusting flames. A lurid luminescence filled the house now. My companion had departed, a mass of falling paper from the library overhead obliterating his slow self-important walk up the stairs. Theses, scripts, new editions of the novels and stories, notes and summaries, first editions and the New York edition, American and English editions – all prepared, as I knew, for the six-parter about his life and the final exposition of his sexual proclivities as shown in the newly discovered (unfinished) story *The Beautiful Child*.

The television programmes are due for transmission October next year. Some parts are already cast with well-known actors. The role of the Master has yet to be filled.

EPILOGUE

Visitors to Lamb House will be pleasantly surprised by the tasteful décor and new panelling throughout the building; they will also be impressed by the cultured woodwork on display in Henry James's study, the small powder room (access through the main reception room: no more than two visitors at a time) where the author's unfinished short story *The Beautiful Child* was discovered, along with the diaries of Theodora Bosanquet and Mary Weld.

Those wishing to acquire the audio of the memoir by Professor Jan Sunderland should place an order in the ground-floor office, once the telephone room. Here it is also possible to search for Bosanquet and Weld on the internet and instigate a search for the relatives of the butler and housekeeper of Mr James's day, Mr and Mrs Smith.

Professor Sunderland's entry in Wikipedia can be found here, this taken up largely by his bibliography of Henry James. The conditions laid down by his estate include the proviso that the last paragraph of the memoir itself must be heard by any visitor to Lamb House interested in supernatural phenomena, both auditory and olfactory (www.orgghostsense/beautifulchild). The last passage of the Professor's memoir may be read online for a fee of £25.

We reproduce a part of it here:

My last visit to Lamb House took place on a winter evening just after Christmas 2011. The newly appointed curator, anxious to meet the last surviving scholar with a direct link to the epoch made famous by Henry James, invited me to wander where I chose in the now-restored and much-cherished retreat of the Master.

This I did, leaving the games of Hide and Seek, the dancing and carol-singing to those who knew nothing of the experiences I had suffered at Rye. To the young guests down in the Garden Room, now a media centre, literature was dead, along with the impossible convoluted style of the long-ago author. I was one of the very few to remember the passionate tone of Mary Weld when she spoke of her employer's melodious voice – and almost certainly the only biographer of the great man to have visited a certain bookshop in Paddington, a year or so after the fire at our rented house at Rye, and purchase Miss Bosanquet's 'ending' to James's unfinished story. I regretted the outlay, of course, when I saw the mishmash received from the 'other side': an amalgam of romantic novelette (Bosanquet) and frankly unbelievable verbal dithering supposedly from James himself. There was no solution to the problem; and if I may be so heartless as to point out that Fanny's twins died in vain, then this has been my sad conclusion.

It was just on midnight on Christmas Eve when, standing on the first-floor landing, I realized the house had become quiet: the guests, hoping for Christmas stockings, had left.

I knew the curator, who slept with his wife in a recently erected bungalow in the grounds, would be happy to unlock the door of the Garden Room so I could wander, one last time, in the place where Henry James had paced, the setting for his inspiration.

But, once there, I lingered – first in the well of the stairs and then, with a sudden sense of my own bravery in conquering fear, by the door of the four-postered room which had been the chamber of the Master.

I heard nothing but the patter of rain, and with the rain, released by the giving and contracting of the wall – who knows? – came the aroma of stale alcohol.

I turned and walked back to the stairs, then out through the hall into the garden. It was a dry evening – the downpour had left no trace – and stars twinkled frostily over the sleeping town.

APPENDIX

From 1896 on, owing to the onset of rheumatism, Henry James was forced to give up writing in longhand. From then onwards he dictated his novels to a secretary who took down his words directly on to a typewriter. The first typist who was with James in this fashion was Mary Weld, who worked with him from 1896 until 1904. Her successor was Theodora Bosanquet. It was she who made the observation that when James struggled with his own convoluted prose style that he 'liked to be able to relieve the tension of a difficult sentence by glancing down the street, sometimes hailing a passing friend from his window, or watching a motorcar pant up the sharp little slope'. During these pauses Miss Bosanquet read a book.

In Rye Henry James was out of reach of most visitors. While he was there he spotted Lamb House, which was built in 1723 by the Mayor of Rye, James Lamb. It opens directly on to a quiet street in the 'little old cobble-stoned, grass-grown, red-roofed town, on the summit of its mildly pyramidal hill', according to the National Trust, the organization that eventually took it over.

The early Georgian house is small, yet elegant, with a wide oak stair, brick walls (red bricks varied with black, giving a deep rose colour), and a nine-foot-high front door. It seemed the answer to his wish for a retreat between May and November. In September 1897 he signed a lease for Lamb House and moved there permanently in June 1898.

In 1900 he acquired the freehold for £2,000.

Not far off were Joseph Conrad, Ford Maddox Ford and the young American Stephen Crane, who provided the stimulus of other writers. It was here, at Lamb House, that Henry James wrote his three late masterpieces, *The Wings of the Dove*, 1902, *The Ambassadors*, 1903, and *The Golden Bowl*, 1904, which earned him his nickname the Master.

Also published by Peter Owen

NINA IN UTOPIA
Miranda Miller

Time travel, Bedlam and the mad Victorian painter Richard Dadd all feature in *Nina in Utopia*. Traumatized by the death of her little daughter in 1854, Nina, the wife of an ambitious doctor, finds herself in London a hundred and fifty years later. As a tourist in the twenty-first century, she believes she has found a Utopia where the grime, poverty and violence of Victorian London have been expunged. She befriends Jonathan, an architect and – shockingly for Nina's Victorian sensibilities – divorcee, who introduces her to the myriad wonders of modern life, including television, curry and clubbing. When she returns to her own time after a long weekend, her husband takes fright on hearing of her experiences and has her committed to Bedlam, where she is a contemporary of the fairy painter Richard Dadd. Here she finds another Utopia in the care of a doctor with modern ideas on patient rehabilitation. Yearning for that magical week-end, however, Jonathan and Nina reach out to one another across the centuries . . .

**PB 978-0-7206-1355-1 • 240pp • £9.95 / EPUB 978-0-7206-1399-5
KINDLE 978-0-7206-1400-8 / PDF 978-0-7206-1401-5**
'A gifted and highly articulate novelist' – *Glasgow Herald*

LOVING MEPHISTOPHELES
Miranda Miller

When Jenny, a third-rate music-hall chanteuse, remarks to her mentor and lover Leo, aka the Great Pantoffsky, that she never wants to grow old, she doesn't know quite who she's speaking to. Her contract to love him will reside at the Metaphysical Bank in High Street Kensington – for ever. As Leo gleefully exploits the rich offerings of twentieth-century London – as a magician, fighter pilot, coke dealer and City banker – Jenny finds that the joy of eternal youth is more ambiguous than one might think. With the strain of constantly having to reinvent herself as her own offspring and watching friends, lovers and family pass, she begins to regret her decision. But it is when she becomes pregnant with a daughter that Leo's true nature and that of her pact is revealed.

**PB 978-0-7206-1275-2 • 312pp • £11.95 / EPUB 978-0-7206-1477-0
KINDLE 978-0-7206-1478-7 / PDF 978-0-7206-1479-4**
'A wonderfully generous novel' – Hilary Mantel

Also published by Peter Owen

THE DARKER SEX
Tales of the Supernatural and Macabre by Victorian Women Writers
Mike Ashley (Ed.)

Ghosts, precognition, suicide and the afterlife are all themes to be found in these thrilling stories by some of the greatest Victorian women writers. It was three women who popularized the Gothic-fiction movement – Clara Reeve, Mary Shelley and Anne Radcliffe – and Victorian women proved they had a talent for creating dark, sensational and horrifying tales. This anthology showcases some of the best work by female writers of the time, including Emily Brontë, Mary Braddon, George Eliot and Edith Nesbit. Mike Ashley contextualizes each story and shows how Victorian women perfected and developed the Gothic genre.

PB 978-0-7206-1335-3 • 248pp • £9.99 / EPUB 978-0-7206-1438-1
KINDLE 978-0-7206-1468-8 / PDF 978-0-7206-1467-1

'A magnificent and terribly readable collection' – BBC Radio 4

'Editor Ashley does his usual fine job in selecting and introducing the eleven entries in a reprint anthology sure to appeal to fans of both Victorian fiction and ghost stories.' – *Publishers Weekly*

THE DREAMING SEX
Early Tales of Scientific Imagination by Women
Mike Ashley (Ed.)

It is a common perception that science fiction is largely the domain of men. Yet the contribution of women should never be underestimated. This book brings together a selection of early science-fiction stories by British and American writers – including Mary Shelley, Harriet Prescott Spofford, Adeline Knapp, Mary E. Braddon, L.T. Meade, Mary Wilkins Freeman, G.M. Barrows, Roquia Sakhawat Hossein, Edith Nesbit, Clotilde Graves, Muriel Pollexfen, Greye La Spina and Clare Winger Harris – and highlights their significance in the early development of the genre and shows the very different angle they cast on the wonders and fears that technological and scientific advances may bring.

PB 978-0-7206-1354-4 • 248pp • £9.99 / EPUB 978-0-7206-1405-3
KINDLE 978-0-7206-1406-0 / PDF 978-0-7206-1407-7

'Tales by some of the most imaginative female genre writers of the Victorian era' – *Sci-Fi* magazine

'A very interesting collection . . . a useful and entertaining addition to the library of the genre's prehistory . . . deserves some considerable attention' – *Foundation*, the journal of the Science-Fiction Foundation

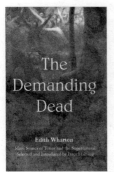

SOME AUTHORS WE HAVE PUBLISHED

James Agee • Bella Akhmadulina • Tariq Ali • Kenneth Allsop
Alfred Andersch • Guillaume Apollinaire • Machado de Assis • Miguel Angel Asturias
Duke of Bedford • Oliver Bernard • Thomas Blackburn • Jane Bowles • Paul Bowles
Richard Bradford • Ilse, Countess von Bredow • Lenny Bruce • Finn Carling
Blaise Cendrars • Marc Chagall • Giorgio de Chirico •Uno Chiyo • Hugo Claus
Jean Cocteau • Albert Cohen • Colette • Ithell Colquhoun • Richard Corson
Benedetto Croce • Margaret Crosland • e.e. cummings • Stig Dalager • Salvador Dalí
Osamu Dazai • Anita Desai • Charles Dickens • Fabián Dobles • William Donaldson
Autran Dourado • Yuri Druzhnikov • Lawrence Durrell • Isabelle Eberhardt
Sergei Eisenstein • Shusaku Endo • Erté • Knut Faldbakken • Ida Fink
Wolfgang George Fischer • Nicholas Freeling • Philip Freund • Carlo Emilio Gadda
Rhea Galanaki • Salvador Garmendia • Michel Gauquelin • André Gide
Natalia Ginzburg • Jean Giono • Geoffrey Gorer • William Goyen • Julien Gracq
Sue Grafton • Robert Graves • Angela Green • Julien Green • George Grosz
Barbara Hardy • H.D. • Rayner Heppenstall • David Herbert • Gustaw Herling
Hermann Hesse • Shere Hite • Stewart Home • Abdullah Hussein
King Hussein of Jordan • Ruth Inglis • Grace Ingoldby • Yasushi Inoue
Hans Henny Jahnn • Karl Jaspers • Takeshi Kaiko • Jaan Kaplinski • Anna Kavan
Yasunuri Kawabata • Nikos Kazantzakis • Orhan Kemal • Christer Kihlman
James Kirkup • Paul Klee • James Laughlin • Patricia Laurent • Violette Leduc
Lee Seung-U • Vernon Lee • József Lengyel • Robert Liddell • Francisco García Lorca
Moura Lympany • Dacia Maraini • Marcel Marceau • André Maurois • Henri Michaux
Henry Miller • Miranda Miller • Marga Minco • Yukio Mishima • Quim Monzó
Margaret Morris • Angus Wolfe Murray • Atle Næss • Gérard de Nerval • Anaïs Nin
Yoko Ono • Uri Orlev • Wendy Owen • Arto Paasilinna • Marco Pallis • Oscar Parland
Boris Pasternak • Cesare Pavese • Milorad Pavic • Octavio Paz • Mervyn Peake
Carlos Pedretti • Dame Margery Perham • Graciliano Ramos • Jeremy Reed
Rodrigo Rey Rosa • Joseph Roth • Ken Russell • Marquis de Sade • Cora Sandel
George Santayana • May Sarton • Jean-Paul Sartre • Ferdinand de Saussure
Gerald Scarfe • Albert Schweitzer • George Bernard Shaw • Isaac Bashevis Singer
Patwant Singh • Edith Sitwell • Suzanne St Albans • Stevie Smith
C.P. Snow • Bengt Söderbergh • Vladimir Soloukhin • Natsume Soseki
Muriel Spark Gertrude Stein • Bram Stoker • August Strindberg
Rabindranath Tagore • Tambimuttu • Elisabeth Russell Taylor • Anne Tibble
Roland Topor • Miloš Urban • Anne Valery • Peter Vansittart • José J. Veiga
Tarjei Vesaas • Noel Virtue • Max Weber • Edith Wharton • William Carlos Williams
Phyllis Willmott • G. Peter Winnington • Monique Wittig • A.B. Yehoshua
Marguerite Young • Fakhar Zaman • Alexander Zinoviev • Emile Zola